THIRTY THREE ™

THE STORY OF HOPE

EDWARD L. FLOM

Prison Book Project
P.O. Box 1146
Sharpes, FL 3

THIRTY THREE

THE STORY OF HOPE

© 2010 Edward L. Flom
All Rights Reserved.

Published by SEI Publishing
Spokane Washington U.S.A.
Printed in U.S.A.

SEI PUBLISHING—is owned and operated by Sound Enterprises, Inc. For more information on the company please visit our website at:
www.SEIzoom.com

All rights reserved. No part of this book may be used or reproduced in any manner whatsoever or stored in any database or retrieval system without written permission except in the case of brief quotations used in critical articles and reviews. Requests for permissions should be addressed to:

SEI Publishing
Nashville Office
177 Marlin Road
White House, TN 37188
info@SEIzoom.com
www.SEIzoom.com

Come explore more about 33 Hope at: www.33Hope.com

ISBN: 978-1-935811-00-8
Jacket Design and Graphics by DIGITAL LIGHTBRIDGE
Book Design Lee Fredrickson

sei publishing

A division of Sound Enterprises, Inc.

Dedication

To my parents, Ed and Beverly, for your
loving support and wise guidance over the years.

To my sons, Taylor and Chandler, for you are my
inspirations in every breath.

And to the one who brought me to the One.

Vignettes

Preface

THIRTY-THREE, THE STORY OF HOPE

On the first week of April, in the year AD 33, a relatively obscure Jewish teacher was tried, brutally beaten, and then crucified by the ruling Roman authorities in the city of Jerusalem. The Rabbi had preached for three years, alongside his twelve disciples, in the villages and rural outposts of Judea and Samaria. These twelve disciples, save the one who betrayed him by identifying him to the authorities, feared for their own lives after seeing their teacher executed and they went into hiding. They were frightened, and their dreams of being witness to the advent of a new Messianic Age were shattered with their Master's crucifixion. Yet, an astonishing series of events would manifest from the moment a highly respected citizen of Jerusalem, Joseph of Arimathea, requested the body of the executed Rabbi for a proper burial. The Roman Governor, Pontius Pilate, promptly granted Joseph's wish. From that very hour in history, a most extraordinary story would unfold.

The Prophet Isaiah 42:1-9
700 BC

"Behold! My Servant whom I uphold,
 My Elect One in whom My soul delights!
I have put My Spirit upon Him;
He will bring forth justice to the Gentiles.
He will not cry out, nor raise His voice,
Nor cause His voice to be heard in the street.
A bruised reed He will not break,
And smoking flax He will not quench;
He will bring forth justice for truth.
He will not fail nor be discouraged,
Till He has established justice in the earth;
and the coastlands shall wait for His law.

Thus, says God the LORD,
Who created the heavens and stretch them out,
Who spread forth the earth and that which comes from it,
Who gives breath to the people on it,
And spirit to those who walk on it:
I, the LORD, have called you to righteousness,
And will hold Your hand;
I will keep You and give You as a covenant to the people,
As a light to the Gentiles,
To open blind eyes,
To bring prisoners from the prison,
Those who sit in darkness from the prison house.
I am the LORD, that is My name;
And My glory I will not give to another,
Nor My praise to carved images.
Behold, the former things have come to pass,
And new things I declare;
Before they spring forth I tell you of them."

The slanted light of the coming sunset passed once across his face. Joseph of Arimathea surmised that he had less than an hour to properly prepare the ravaged body for a burial in accordance with the Law. The body lay lifelessly beneath him. It was written, in the tradition of Moses, that those who had been hanged should be buried by nightfall, so as not to defile the land. Ordinarily, he would have had plenty of time to complete the task at hand, but the Sabbath would commence at sunset and signal the beginning of the Passover remembrance. Joseph would celebrate with his family, alongside thousands of pilgrims who had come to the city with tender, spring lambs to sacrifice to the God of Abraham at the Holy Temple. Shortly after the Rabbi's death from crucifixion that very afternoon, Joseph had gone before the Roman Procurator of Judea, Pontius Pilate, to request the body for a proper Jewish burial. He had been surprised when his wish was granted. After all, it was the normal practice of the Romans to let the crucified bodies of its enemies rot upon the cross to serve as a lasting example to the people they ruled. But Joseph had heard the parables and the simple teachings of Rabbi Jesus of Nazareth, as the broken body beneath him was called—he could not allow the shame of seeing his body tossed into the shared grave of the rotting criminals. Something in those spoken words had moved his heart and had filled him with the courage to make such a bold request to Pilate. As a prominent member of the ruling Sanhedrin Council, Joseph had futilely argued with the High Priest, Caiaphas, to spare the Rabbi's life in the early morning trial. But no one in all of Jerusalem had the power to save the charismatic Rabbi after he answered, "I am," when specifically questioned by Caiaphas, if he was Christ the Messiah, the Son of God. Moving swiftly now, Joseph unfolded a linen cloth that he had purchased during the day to serve as a burial shroud. He tore the cloth into strips to bind and properly wrap the body, and then left a square yard to cover the Rabbi's face. A servant brought him a sponge-laden cask of water from the cistern at the foot of Golgotha, so that he could begin the cleansing—still, he was without the traditional burial spices to anoint the body by Jewish custom. However, he did own a family tomb nearby where he could place the Rabbi and allow his body to naturally decay to bones. Joseph would be able to collect those bones in a few weeks and place them in a limestone ossuary to be given to Jesus of Nazareth's absent family from Galilee. It was the least he could do. After all, there is such deep shame in being buried alone and not in one's family's tomb. He deserved a proper burial. So, Joseph of Arimathea set his full attention on his appointed task as the afternoon sun skittered amidst the rocky cliffs at the foot of the Hill of Skulls.

Squinting, Joseph took full measure of the body that lay beneath him. The Rabbi's shoulders had been wrenched from their sockets so that his arms hung limply from mid chest. There were nail wounds in each hand that had surely been ripped open by the weight of his body hanging on the cross. The Rabbi's back was shredded with savage wounds inflicted earlier in the day. They had used whips and flaying instruments with metal bits of bent nails that were perfectly designed to cleave the skin of the accused and leave the exposed muscle gaping underneath. There were larger nail-hole shafts in each foot that extended through his mangled heels. And on the left side of the exposed rib cage was a jagged pink wound; it was splayed open and dripping a clear fluid upon the reddish-caked stains of the dried blood that clung stubbornly to the corpse. There were deep cuts in the scalp and most of his teeth were either gone or broken into exposed fragments hiding behind distended lips. One eye was swollen completely shut and the other stared vacantly at Joseph. It was on the swollen eye that he began the cleaning, and gently pressed the sponge against the Rabbi's face when he saw the stooped gait of an older man approaching him in the center of the falling sun. "Joseph," said Nicodemus the Pharisee, "I have been looking for you. See, I have come with spices."

The old man was lugging a lambskin bag behind him and it was dragging in the dust. "Look at him, my friend," said Joseph, "look at what the Romans have done to him."

Nicodemus grimaced as his eyes glanced down at the body. A deep sigh seemed to collapse his chest upon itself and he shook his head with great sorrow. "Do not blame only the Romans, Joseph," he said in a voice that whistle cracked with age, "for it was our own Sanhedrin that tried and convicted him this morning. And the people of Jerusalem—they called for his blood. No one, I tell you, is innocent of this abomination. Not one soul." Nicodemus set the bag to the side of the wooden ladder that held the Rabbi's body. He pulled back the drawstring so that Joseph could lift out the aloes and the myrrh—plenty enough to apply to all of the torn strips. Joseph continued to sponge clean the body and Nicodemus began to work with the energy of a younger man.

"But, Nicodemus, how are we to blame?" Joseph cried. "We both spoke for him before the Sanhedrin this morning. How could we have defended him against the High Priest, Caiaphas, after the Rabbi admitted to his blasphemy? What man could make such a claim—to openly say that he is the Son of God and, therefore, as divine as our Holy God?" The blood and the water dripped off the Rabbi's body and formed red rivulets in the dust beneath their feet.

For a long time, the old man did not answer. Joseph worked diligently in the silence, and soon the Rabbi's wounds glistened pink against the scourged flesh. Together, they folded his arms across his chest and tied them in place about the wrists with a taut strip of linen. They gingerly secured his jaw by encircling a linen strip beneath his chin and around the crown of his head. Joseph lifted the Rabbi's feet in the air so that Nicodemus could wrap the body from the feet to just underneath the folded arms. They would have to move quickly, and then command a few of Joseph's servants to help them carry the prepared body to the tomb.

Nicodemus broke the silence with the softest of voices. "Joseph, I am going to tell you something that will cost me my life if it becomes known." Joseph nodded his affirmation without looking up. "I went to see this Jesus of Nazareth, in secret, two years ago during the Passover season to ask him one simple question. I went to him under the cover of darkness." Nicodemus hesitated and allowed a group of chattering youths to pass. "I said to him, 'Rabbi, I know that you are a teacher that has come from God, for no man can do the signs that you do unless God is with him. I am an old man and my spirit is tired. Please, Rabbi, tell me how I can enter the Kingdom of God?'"

Joseph clapped for his nearby servants and ordered them to carry the Rabbi's prepared body to the burial tomb. The servants lifted the ends of the wooden ladder and, when they moved out of hearing distance, Joseph fell into step with Nicodemus and said, "Please, go on."

"He said to me, 'How is it that a Pharisee like you does not know the answer?' But before I could protest, with both hands outstretched, he took hold of my shoulders and said, 'I tell you the truth, unless one is born again, one cannot see the Kingdom of God.' 'Born again?' I asked him, 'Teacher, how can one enter his mother's womb for a second time?'" The old man smiled and his teeth glinted through his white beard as he recalled the memory. Joseph placed a hand on Nicodemus's shoulder for the servants had reached the entrance to his tomb. Together, the two men gently reached down to touch the bloodless cheeks of the Rabbi before placing the linen shroud into place to cover his face. Joseph ordered the men to go inside and to place the Rabbi's body on a narrow, stone slab that had been carved out of the rock face in the back of the tomb.

Nicodemus turned to Joseph and grabbed the younger man's hands and brought Joseph's right ear very close to his mouth. "Joseph of Arimathea," he whispered, "he said that one must be born again in the spirit, like the wind, to enter the Kingdom of Heaven." Nicodemus grimaced as if his words were painful for him to say. "And then he told me that he was the Son of God, sent by his Father to save the world from evil, and that those who believe in him will not perish but will have eternal life."

Joseph did not respond right away, as the four servants had returned to the entrance. Each of the four, grabbed a branch and placed it under a round rock to push it forward to seal the entrance of the tomb. This stone would protect the body from scavenging animals, and save those who would pass near the tomb in the coming days from the rotting smell of decay. Joseph joined his men in pushing and rolling the heavy rock into place until the edges set smooth through the opening. As the tomb closed to darkness, he caught a glimpse of two women cautiously observing their actions from behind a row of date palms on the hill above the tomb. Despite their movements to remain hidden to his glance, he recognized one of them as Mary of Magdala, a known devotee and supporter of the Rabbi. It had been rumored that the wandering Jesus has banished seven demons from her two years before. Joseph knew that she had traveled with him and his closest disciples since that day. Her long dark hair was disheveled about her sullen face, which was streaked with tears of despair. Had Jesus also said these things to her?

He let his gaze leave Mary, and released the servants, before turning to look directly at the old man to ask, "And, so, do you believe in him, my friend?" The silence hung heavily in the dying dusk. "Nicodemus, tell me," Joseph demanded, while searching the older man's face to see the truth, "do you truly believe that we have allowed the murder of the Messiah of our own people?"

The old man did not answer. Joseph heard only the murmured chants of fervent prayers and the faint sounds of faraway music. The Holy Sabbath had begun and Jerusalem was awash with devout pilgrims joyously making their way to pray inside the walls of the Temple.

The High Priest, Caiaphas, watched as the setting sun dipped below the polished garden wall in the plush courtyard of his father-in-law's home. He had not been to sleep since he arose from his bed on Wednesday morning and his exhaustion was carved into his bearded face. What a day today had been! His men had sought, and found, the scandalous Nazarene last evening and placed him on trial in the early morning, while the moon was still shining brightly in its fullness. "Thanks be to Judas Iscariot for his accurate information on the whereabouts of this charlatan and the band of ignorant Galileans who rarely left his side." He was thankful, too, that Pontius Pilate had finally granted the Council of the Sanhedrin's wish for the crucifixion of the blasphemous Rabbi Jesus. The Romans allowed the Sanhedrin to govern the affairs of their people; nonetheless, only an officer of Pilate's position could authorize a capital punishment. "What did the Romans know about living in obedience under the laws of a powerful God? Nothing! They are only concerned with their wealth and pleasures of the flesh. Guilty, this one, and no different than the rest of those traveling frauds who claimed to be the Divine Messiah, and deceived the common people with their cunning tricks and signs," he continued in his thought. Virtually all of the priests of the Sadducees, the Essenes, and the Pharisees that served in his High Council had agreed with Caiaphas' thinking on this matter. "After all, as he had said to all of them at the trial, 'It was better for one man to die, rather than to witness the whole of their people massacred by the Romans.' Neither Pilate, nor Rome, would tolerate an insurrection from their subjects." The fanciful tales regarding that charismatic Rabbi had brought great excitement to the common people. There were fascinating stories of the blind seeing, the lame walking, and even the dead rising from their tombs to proclaim this man's greatness. "Ah, but the Sadducees don't believe in such nonsense—there are no angels, and resurrection from death is preposterous. And now, Jerusalem is teeming with dangerous passions and rebels of all types stirred up by these crazy stories. It is a tinderbox, one spark away from bursting into flames."

Caiaphas allowed his thoughts to tarry about the decision that had been made in the morning of that day. "Had not this self proclaimed Messiah even aligned himself with the Zealots who spoke of attacking the Romans and seizing Jerusalem by force? No, no, no, this cannot be—at least the Romans allow us to worship the God of Abraham and to live without interference to the precepts of our Law. How could he, the High Priest of Jerusalem, appointed by those very same Romans, have allowed such a dangerous pretender to go about preaching those childlike, confusing sermons that so directly threatened his position in Jerusalem?" It had thrilled him to see how the mob, the easily influenced rabble, had turned on the Rabbi after welcoming him into Jerusalem on the last Sunday with a greeting fit for a King. "Well, this imposter was no King! And he was certainly no Messiah! The real coming Messiah would not allow himself to be nailed to a cross like a common criminal by the heathen Romans. The Anointed One will lead our people to a spectacular victory over the Romans and return God's chosen people to their rightful place in the hierarchy of nations.

Clearly, the coming Messiah would possess the full strength and power of God, Himself. Yes, the long awaited Messiah, from the House of David, was coming; and it was certainly not this blasphemous schlemiel that spoke in riddles and childish parables and carried about with the ignorant scum of Galilee. It was best for everyone that this Jesus of Nazareth, of all places—that forsaken, filthy desert outpost—laid dead in the common burial pit at Golgotha amongst the other criminals who deserved his same fate."

"Now," Caiaphas noted, with some satisfaction, "I am free to preside over the Passover in remembrance of the days of Moses; a time in history when an angry God had unleashed the tenth plague on the people of Egypt by ordering the death of the firstborn son in every home. It was a time honored story of how the Lord had instructed the Israelites, His chosen people, to mark the doorposts of their homes with the blood of spring lambs; and that the spirit of the Lord would pass over those homes and save their firstborn sons from destruction." That day, at almost the exact moment that the Nazarene was breathing his last breath in Golgotha, he had presided over the sacrifice of the paschal lamb in the four ceremonies on the altar of the Temple. It was his solemn responsibility as the High Priest to execute the paschal lamb while the Levites chanted the Hallel, the Psalms of the Passover. He was a descendant of those who have always protected them. The people of Israel had been saved then, and it was his sacred duty as their High Priest, to do whatever was required of him to save them once again from the likes of those who would fill their ignorant heads with false hopes and utter blasphemies in the face of the great God of Abraham.

He was content with his decision, and gathered his robe for his walk to the Temple, when his thoughts were interrupted by the swollen voice of his father-in-law, Annas, who had served as the previous High Priest before Caiaphas had received his revered appointment from Rome. "Caiaphas, my son," the robust patriarch intoned, "let us walk to the Temple together. There is a matter that I wish to discuss with you." Caiaphas greeted him and quickened his step to remain besides his still vigorous father-in-law. Annas was an enormously wealthy man, and many in the city of Jerusalem still considered him to be its most powerful citizen. He did not suffer fools gladly and remained an intimidating figure at the Temple. He could destroy the confidence of a younger priest who had failed to properly grasp a sweeping understanding of the Torah and the Law. The previous Roman Procurator, Valerius Gratus, had removed him from the High Priest position in AD 15, but the Israelites still gave him the full respect afforded to the one who presided over the Sanhedrin. "I have come to understand that Joseph of Arimathea was given the body of the Nazarene this afternoon, by Pontius Pilate, for a proper burial in his personal tomb near Golgotha," Annas said in his sonorous voice. "Are you aware of this, my son?"

"No, father, I was not," replied Caiaphas.

"Well, then, Caiaphas," Annas continued, "are you aware of the rantings of the Nazarene and what his disciples have said within the very gates of our Temple." The old man came to a halt and stared firmly into the eyes of his son-in-law. He knew Caiaphas to be a clever and ruthless man who would not lightly discard the gift of experience. "It is said that this rebellious fool, this false Messiah, has promised to rise from the dead in three days hence."

"Please father, listen to yourself. Do you want to give any credence to such a preposterous claim? I cannot imagine why Joseph of Arimathea requested such a thing—and we will ask him that very question before the Sanhedrin—but I saw the coming death of the Rabbi, myself, at the foot of his cross before we left to sacrifice the paschal lamb. I can witness to you that he is most assuredly as dead as stone," said Caiaphas, with just a touch of exasperation.

"Of course, my son, and you know that I do not give a whisper of credence to the foolish superstitions of these charlatans," Annas replied. "Still, though, what is to stop his motley group of Galileans from stealing the body in the dead of the night and claiming that, behold—he has risen from the dead? They could say that he is walking among us and enjoying our wine as they claimed, without witness for Lazarus, in Bethany."

Caiphas allowed his mind to wander, "Ah yes, the ludicrous tale of Lazarus that had been sweeping through the streets of Jerusalem. A quick spreading rumor about how the Rabbi had raised Lazarus of Bethany from the dead after he had lain in his family's tomb for four days. Such nonsense! The man staggered about into the arms of his loved ones wrapped in burial rags and reeking with the smell of death. Still, it was true these rebels could certainly inspire an insurrection against the Romans if they went about claiming that the Rabbi had raised this Lazarus from the dead and then defied his very own death! This kind of silly babble could take hold with the people and put the ruling Sanhedrin at great risk."

In a flash, Caiaphas understood. His clever father-in-law had a clear point—the legitimacy of the Nazarene's claims would not be disproved by just the indisputable fact of his witnessed death. No, he would have to decay into white bones before the rabble would fully accept that he was just another false Messiah in a long line of disappointments. There would be a new one in the summer, claiming signs and performing magic tricks like a jester in Herod's court.

Caiaphas sighed with a deep tiredness and turned to speak to his father-in-law. "Father, I see your point. You are to be commended for keeping such a sharp mind and holding your wisdom so close at hand. What do you suggest we do?" said the smiling High Priest, who suspected that the powerful Annas had a plan in mind.

Annas pondered his response as they came upon the Temple. The smell of the burnt offerings of the young spring lambs hung invitingly in the air. Fathers and sons moved with excitement in every direction as they entered the Temple to pray and commemorate the Passover. The bearded men showed deference to the two of them by clearing their path and pointing them out to their younger sons. "Caiaphas, do you see the young Pharisee near the column over there?" Annas asked as Caiaphas's eyes scanned the portico. "Yes, that one—Saul, right over there—he is small in stature but was very well educated in the Torah at the foot of our learned friend, Rabbi Gamaliel. Gamaliel told me that he was his finest student; an excellent scribe who has a splendid future before him." When he was sure that Caiaphas saw the diminutive Saul, he went on, and carefully lowered his voice to say, "Go and take the young man with you, along with a few others, to meet with Governor Pilate in the outside entry way of Herod's Palace near the Citadel. He will be dining there tonight. Ask him to post some guards and place a Roman Governor's seal around the tomb where our Joseph of Arimathea has buried this Jesus. This should deter anyone from disturbing the body of our sleeping Messiah," he said with a voice tinged with derision.

"But the Sabbath has begun," Caiaphas said in response. "You know that we are to make no such requests on the Sabbath of the Passover. And what makes you think, Father, that Pilate will even hear this request, much less grant it?"

Annas knelt before the High Priest, and Caiaphas extended his blessing by praying over the head of the patriarch. When he was finished, Annas looked up and a gentle smile escaped through the white strands of his twisting beard that matched a twinkling in the old man's eyes. "Lay aside your worries, Caiaphas, and go quickly; for all has been arranged. There are a few things that must remain unknown to even the High Priest of Jerusalem."

A woman's wail pierced the night air at the entrance of the Rabbi's tomb. Mary of Magdela had bid farewell to the Rabbi's Aunt, Mary, wife of Cleopas, a few hours hence, when the servants of Joseph of Arimathea had rolled a rock into place to close Jesus' tomb. She and Mary had watched Joseph and Nicodemus hastily prepare her Lord's body for burial before the Sabbath had come. Aunt Mary had told her that she would walk back alone into the city to find the disciple John and her sister, Jesus' mother. But Mary Magdalene could not move. A wrenching pain that had emptied her stomach onto the ground overcame her; and it sent sharp daggers into her chest that stole her very breath. A pain that had gripped her in the morning, as she witnessed the vicious public scourging of her Master, and had only grown in severity as she had stood underneath his cross and heard him cry out his final words. She moaned with a bottomless grief and dug her fingertips into the soft dirt at the entrance. "Why," she screamed silently to herself, "why did they kill her Rabbi? Why did they murder this beautiful man?"

The Magdalene had first seen the Rabbi in the spring, two years hence. At that time, she was a young woman of nineteen years, possessed of seven demons, and each fought for dominance on a scarred battlefield in the center of her tortured soul. A remembrance of her sins passed before her eyes—the immoralities, the screaming timbre of her rages, and the hatred that welled up inside of her until she spit it out like poisonous venom when it reached the level of her lips. She had glanced out the window of her home on that day in May, and had seen the Rabbi sitting as still as a Roman statue in the shade of a cypress tree. He was alone. Mary stormed across the beaten down sand, intending to scream at the trespasser and banish him from her property, but found that she could not speak when her eyes met his gaze. Those eyes had mesmerized her, and she had been startled by the kindness that shown from his countenance.

"Miriam," he had said onto her, calling her by her given name even though he was a stranger in Magdala. She had wanted to slap him for being so ill mannered, but her feet had remained frozen in their place. The stranger had brought his hands together in front of his robe and smiled at her.

"How could this meddlesome wanderer have come to know my given name?" she thought.

And Jesus had said to her, "I understand that you have many admirers." She had formed the words with her tongue to tell him to leave immediately, but no sound had come forth from her mouth. The demons inside of her seemed to recognize that man, and none moved nor spoke. "And some of them see themselves in you and love you for themselves—and some love you for your beauty," he continued.

At last, she had found her voice and had been able to confront him with a flash of anger. "And what business is it of yours to inquire about who I wish to entertain," she had snarled. But even as she spoke, an unrequested peace had come to gnaw at the edges of her hatred and she had felt the frightened demons squirming with unease in her body as they sought a path to escape.

Mary stared at the round rock in front of the Rabbi's tomb. She wanted to be strong enough to move it and go to her Master. Nicodemus had brought aloe and myrrh, but there was more that she could do for her teacher. She looked into the sky and prayed to her Almighty God to allow her to serve her Master once again, to wash his feet and anoint him with precious oils. Crying quietly, her thoughts harkened back to that wondrous day of her first encounter with the Rabbi.

All of her anger had left her when she had felt that peace. All at once, she had understood that she was face to face with an extraordinary man and she wanted to know more about him. "Will you come into my home and share some bread and wine with me," she had demurely asked of the traveling Rabbi. "I will introduce you to my father."

Jesus had risen to his feet. "No," he said while preparing to go about his way, "but know this, my sister. I love you in yourself. Your beauty will most assuredly fade in the autumn of your days, but I will always love the unseen in you."

Mary had been astonished. She did not speak a word as the Rabbi walked away with a walk like no other man— his sandals skimming the dust and his back as straight as if a Roman spear had been thrown down the length of his spine and directly into the ground. She had watched him walk down the path that led away from her family home until he was joined by a throng of others who had been waiting for his arrival. It was at that exact moment that she perceived her destiny. The seven demons had left her as quickly as they had come; there remained no one inside of her but her own grateful soul. A tremendous feeling washed over her, liberating her from her tarnished past. She joined Jesus and his disciples the very next day, and had walked with him for the last two years, caring for him and the others, and listening to each of his parables and teachings with the innocence of a young child.

And now she was punching her fists into the sand at the entrance of his tomb. "He is dead!—Gone away!—Murdered!" She called out to him in her despair, but heard only silence. Yet, even in the dark of that evening, she knew that she could not leave him. Mary Magdalene wailed in her grief well past midnight, until she finally fell asleep in the wet sand in a moment between the whimpers of her shredded voice and the breaking of her heart.

The young Pharisee, Saul of Tarsus, sat amidst of a group of men who were listening to the treasured and broadminded words of the learned Rabbi Gamaliel, under a column in the south portico of the Temple, when the High Priest, Caiaphas, came upon them. Rabbi Gamaliel was the most prominent rabbinic teacher in all of Jerusalem, and Saul was a strong enough student to be sitting in the honored seat directly to the right of the wizened rabbi. The men were engaged in a lively discussion, about the ancient tribe of Benjamin, when Caiaphas interrupted their repartee with a whispered word to the revered Rabbi. Gamaliel listened carefully and then motioned to Saul to rise and take his leave to speak with the High Priest.

Saul could not imagine what the High Priest could want from him, but he bowed respectfully and inquired, "Rabbi Caiaphas, may I be of service to you?"

Caiaphas took hold of the young man just above the elbow of his left arm and guided Saul into a private antechamber at the end of the portico. The High Priest closed the door behind them and motioned for Saul to take a seat in front of an ornate desk carved out of a glistening marble. He lit a long, white candle to illuminate the room.

Saul sat with some trepidation as the High Priest cleared his throat to speak. "Saul of Tarsus, your teacher speaks very highly of you."

"Rabbi Caiaphas," Saul replied, "it is I that am honored by his teachings. My father has given me Roman citizenship but I am an Israelite first, and Rabbi Gamaliel has instilled in my heart the wisdom of our Hebrew Scriptures, our Torah, the Law.

I have committed my life to the God of Israel, not the Emperor of Rome."

"Perhaps Annas was correct in selecting this young man," Caiaphas said to himself. He could see a glowing intelligence and a focused intensity in the Grecian features of the bantam redhead that sat before him. "I shall invite Saul to celebrate the second Seder at Annas' home, for those unable to be with us last evening, when the sun sets tonight. Annas will enjoy testing the young Pharisee on the customs of their ancestors."

The High Priest settled back in his chair and inquired, "Saul, do you know of this Rabbi Jesus of Nazareth?"

"Yes, my lord, the one who was crucified today in Golgotha," Saul acknowledged.

"Yes, the very one," said the High Priest before continuing. "There are members of our Council who had concerns with the rantings of this crucified Rabbi and his band of devoted Galileans. Have you ever heard him preach at the Temple?"

"I heard him speak on Tuesday of this week, my lord, the day after he caused quite a ruckus with the moneychangers in the Temple," answered Saul without offering any opinion of the Rabbi's preaching.

The High Priest could see that the young scribe was nervous. To calm him, he leaned forward conspiratorially and said, "Saul, do not fear these questions. Please lay aside your fear—we are just two men talking." Saul breathed a barely audible sigh of relief that did not go unnoticed by the High Priest. Satisfied, Caiaphas went on to say, "Please, without fear of retribution, tell me what you truly felt about this man? Do you believe that he was a holy man, or a clever charlatan, a magician?"

Saul looked at the powerful High Priest as the light from the candle lit his distinguishly featured face. He knew that Caiaphas had been the High Priest in Jerusalem for fifteen years now, and that they were not just two men talking. This man held the power to have him stoned outside of the gates of the Temple

24

with the witness of another man and a wave of his hand. Still, he decided to tell the truth—his real feelings. The young Pharisee was smart enough to know that his life was about to change in one way or the other, and brave enough to see in which way it would turn. "My lord," Saul began, "there is no question in my mind that this Rabbi was an extraordinary man. He was born in David's city, Bethlehem, but spent his days as a lowly Nazarene. Yet, he spoke with such eloquence about the prophets of our people, and on the most subtle aspects of our Law. There is no question as to the brilliance of his mind and the power of his ideas. I heard even a deep confidence in his voice, a calming peace, that seemed to mesmerize his audience."

"Please, go on," said Caiaphas.

"Nonetheless, I saw his words and his teachings as a mortal threat to our Law. It is not that he claimed to be the Messiah—I found that more foolish than blasphemous," said a more confident Saul. "No, my real concern was that he wished to shift the central focus of our worship away from the Law and our reverence of the Temple. Does this not strike at the very heart of all that we hold dear as the people of Israel, my lord? I ask you, what are we without the Law of our ancestors, of Abraham and of Moses? How would we differ from the Godless pagans if we turned away from our pious ways and our devout communion in our Holy Temple?"

The High Priest signaled his agreement. Annas, as usual, had been quite astute to sense the passionate intelligence that flowed from the mouth of that fine young man. He explained to Saul that powerful voices in the Sanhedrin wished to make sure that the revolutionary words of the itinerant Rabbi would lie quietly beside him for all of eternity in the darkness of his tomb. He asked the young man if he would accompany him later to Herod's Palace. They would be among a select group making a request to Pontius Pilate to post Roman guards and a Governor's seal at the entrance of the tomb. This would insure, he explained to the rapt young man from Tarsus, that the ignorant Galileans would be unable to steal the body and make any ludicrous claims in the days ahead.

The light shimmered from the candle and made shadows on the walls as the two of them discussed the very real threat that the preachings of that Jesus posed to their devout community. Their conversation continued on for a few moments more until only one question remained unanswered. "Saul, my son," said Caiaphas, "I have a serious question to ask you. You may say yes, or you may say no, and go on about your way after we return from our visit with Governor Pilate. Of course, if you choose to answer no, then I will implore you keep our conversation, and our plans, private between us." Saul quickly gestured his acceptance. The High Priest prepared to extinguish the candle in anticipation of their walk together to see Pilate through the crooked streets of Jerusalem. "We are seeking a man who will search out, and keep a close eye on any followers of this blasphemous and dangerous Rabbi. I know that you understand that we cannot allow this man's ideas to take hold among our people. You will have my full support in this endeavor, and I will offer you, without question, the monies that you will need to search out anyone who sees this dead Rabbi as a martyr. You will report your findings to me, until everyone who swears allegiance to this man is silenced or leaves our Holy Jerusalem." The High Priest blew out the candle and cracked the door into the portico so that both men could see the prayerful activity of their people as they worshiped together in the Temple. Caiaphas, with great seriousness, turned to face the young Pharisee to ask, "Are you this man?"

The curling red loops of Saul's untethered hair danced in affirmation as he nodded to the High Priest and said, "Indeed, I am."

The disciple, John, awoke early in the morning on the day after the crucifixion of his Rabbi Jesus, with the moon still shining brightly on the hushed streets of Jerusalem. For just a brief moment, he thought that the events of yesterday were perhaps only a bad dream; but as his grogginess cleared, his grief thrashed within him once again. Jesus of Nazareth was dead. His Master had been crucified on a Roman cross—beaten, flogged, ridiculed, and pierced until dead. Yes, it had happened—John had personally witnessed the ferocity of the Roman soldiers as they had hammered nails into Jesus' hands and feet, and then had lifted him into the sky to die. He had seen, with his own eyes, each of the indignities that Jesus had suffered yesterday, and had been completely powerless to intervene. John rose to a sitting position and began to bind his feet into his sandals. He raised his coarse robe over his head and let it cascade downward over his thinning torso. He was thirty two years old, hungry and afraid, and saddened to the very core of his soul. He had not seen his Master take his final breath, nor heard his last words. John had been the only one of the Rabbi's twelve disciples who had walked among the crowd the whole of the way as they took Jesus, bearing the cross himself, to the place called the place of a skull, where he had been put to death. He had watched as Jesus endured insults and mockery while nailed to a cross, alongside two guilty criminals who were crucified with him. He had watched as Jesus absorbed all the violence of the soldiers, only to transform that violence into love as he, from the depths of his own pain, reached out to comfort the repentant thief who was crucified next to him.

Breathing in, John realized that he held no contempt for his fellow disciples, for their lives were as threatened as their Master's, and the Romans would have been only too happy to add a few more crosses to the ones that despoiled the horizon of the rolling, desert hills. Even Peter the burly leader, and the bravest of the Twelve, and whose sword could still swing in righteous anger, had left Jesus alone to face his fate. But John had not been able to take his leave and abandon Jesus on that sorrowful day. No, he would have comforted him all the way unto his death had not the Master spoken to him from the cross.

A grimacing Jesus had looked down upon where John was standing with Mary, and Mary of Magdala, and had said to them with a voice that found its way through his pain, "Woman, behold your son!" The two women, weeping and shattered with despair, had walked with Jesus during every moment of his final day. Hearing those words, Mary had collapsed into John's arms and the disciple had wrapped her into the loose linings of his brown robe. If he had not supported her with his arms, then he was sure that she would have collapsed into the dirt.

And then, John remembered, Jesus had looked to him with eyes that bore the clearest intention and said, "Behold your mother." John had understood. After all, he had spent the last three years of his life wandering about Galilee with this man, and eleven other disciples, as they witnessed the signs and miracles that their Master had performed. Still, it was not always easy to understand the true meaning of the Master's words, for he often spoke in parables and answered questions with questions. The Twelve had been frequently perplexed by their teacher's decisions and the paths that he had chosen. "How had this happened to him? My brother James and I are just simple fishermen, content with our simple lives. We are good men, but not ready to die in this strange city so far from our boats and our families," thought John. This time, though, John had understood Jesus' wish with full clarity, and he had gathered Mary in his arms and led her away from her son's crucifixion to return to the safe haven of his young friend, Mark's family home.

All of the Galileans had been staying there for the last

week, in the upper room of the home, under a slanted ceiling. The other women—Aunt Mary, Salome, Joanna—had tended to Mother Mary's grief, rocking and wailing with her as they held her in their arms. Ah, if only the wailing of women could truly lift the burdens of one's grief! Now, before even the roosters had stirred, John looked about the room and saw the shadowed shapes of the women and his brother, James, fast asleep on pillows and lambskin rugs and blankets bunched together on the opposite sides of the long, wooden table where they took their meals. "Where are the others, and where is our leader, the bold and courageous Peter?" John thought to himself.

John finished with the last bind of his left sandal and then looked closely at his foot bound inside of the leather straps. The sight of his foot jolted him back to the last dinner that the disciples had shared with their Master in that very room. The Rabbi had known, and prophesied, about his coming demise to the men in attendance. Jesus had not run from his fate, but instead, had ordered a cask of water to be brought to him so that he could clean the feet of his disciples. Kneeling before a protesting Peter, Jesus had said, "What I am doing, you do not understand now, but you will know after this."

John remembered that Peter had said to his Rabbi, "You shall never wash my feet." But the Nazarene had rebuked him by threatening to allow Peter no part of himself until the headstrong fisherman had acquiesced.

John would never forget the beauty that had shone from the Master's face as he washed each of the disciple's feet, and then turned to them to say, "You call me Teacher and Lord, and you say well, for so I am. If I then, your Lord and Teacher, have washed your feet, you also ought to wash another one's feet; for I have given you an example that you should do as I have done to you."

And now John looked down upon his dusty foot as a tear of his grief splashed down to reveal a drop of cleansed skin. This man was gone from his life now, leaving only these remembered moments and the perplexing parables that the Rabbi had used to teach them along their journey. "I will remember him, just as he asked at our last meal together, I promise. When I eat bread, I will eat it in remembrance of his body, and when I drink wine, I will drink it in remembrance of his blood, the blood that spurted out of his side when he was speared by a Roman soldier at his cross yesterday afternoon, the blood of the slaughtered lamb. At least I have these gifts to take back to me to Galilee. Yes, at least I have these lessons, these moments."

The young disciple rose to his feet on trembling legs. And where was Mary Magdalene? Was she still with the Master at the cross? Despite a growing fear that fluttered and danced in the pit of his empty stomach, John slowly descended the stairs into the main room and shut the side door quietly behind him. The front door was always locked, and only opened when an agreed upon knock was heard. He took a deep breath and surveyed the descending street for Roman soldiers. Seeing none, he took a quick step between the scurrying hens and over the slats of a wooden fence to make his way back to Golgotha under the safety of the murky dawn. He was a pious young man, and he knew it was wrong to travel on the Sabbath, but his task on that morning was taking him down the empty streets upon which he tread. He was sure of the path and his duty, at that moment, to his crucified Master—to find the Magdalene before the first light of that morning and bring her back to the safety of the home, even if he was to do it on the holiest of Sabbaths.

The black bearded Peter tore the pit of an olive out with his teeth and spit it upon the ground. He allowed the juice from the fruit to run down his chin and into his matted beard. No one could see him hidden here in his shame—sitting in the shadow of an olive tree in a grove perched high above Jerusalem, on the west side of the Mount of Olives, just off the road to Bethany. But from that vantage point, he could clearly see the places that had borne his shame. He pushed the branches apart with his hands to look over the valley. "There, the Garden of Gethsemane, where I fell asleep like a child when Jesus asked me to pray with him, in his moment of greatest need. The man I loved more than any in the world had come to me to seek comfort in his time of crisis, and I fell asleep instead," thought Peter.

He could see the roof top of the treacherous Annas' house, where he had denied even knowing Jesus three times in the early morning of yesterday's light, just as his master had told him he would do in their last supper together. "Three times," Jesus had told him, "three times you will deny me before the rooster crows twice."

He had denied his Master! The Messiah! He had been fearful of being exposed by a simple, servant girl who questioned him in the courtyard of Annas' home. "What kind of spineless rodent am I? For this cowardice, I have brought curses upon myself forever. With this shame, how can I ever face the others? Yes, the big, brave Peter who the Twelve look to for guidance and to build up their own courage; but I am truly nothing more that a whimpering deserter who ran away from the first threat of exposure. How fraudulent my courage—how fragile my faith, and now," he mumbled to himself, "how weakened is my reputation and command?"

Peter tore at the front of his robe and clasped his hands about his face with ringing slaps of self-hatred. A drop of blood dripped from the tip of his thumb and he mixed its salty flavor with the olive juice swirling beneath his tongue. He looked over the wall to the north of the city to where he assumed they had taken Jesus for the crucifixion. Of that he was not completely sure, for he had escaped the city the previous morning and ran to that very spot where he had spent a sleepless night. Smoke from the first fires of the morning rose into the air above the barren hills above Golgotha, the land of the forgotten skulls. Peter twisted in the knowledge that he had not stood with his Master—believed in him, loved him, and gone to even his own death with him as a testament to his devotion. "No, I ran as fast as a frightened rabbit out of the city gates, when I was discovered, to save my own, worthless skin. A skin that now stretched too taut about a body bloated with the bile of my own disgust." The vision of a crucified Jesus tore across his mind. "How could this Messiah, the mighty One, sent by God himself, allow himself to be nailed on a cross like a thief, by the heathen Romans? Why, with just a wave of his hand, he could have defeated Pilate's soldiers and taken his rightful place upon the throne of Israel. I have witnessed countless miracles since the day Jesus had called me to follow. Even Lazarus had risen four days after his death, and staggered out of his tomb clad in burial rags into the loving arms of his joyous family, when called to rise by Jesus." He shook his head violently to understand, but he could not grasp the Lord's remarkable decision to allow his own crucifixion. In his exhaustion, Peter made himself a bed of olive leaves at the base of the tree. He pulled a broken branch down over himself to conceal his prostrate form from prying eyes. Perhaps some sleep would replenish the potency he would need to return and face the others in his shame.

In the dreamy state before his sleep overtook him, he remembered the moment when he knew that the Nazarene was the One. Jesus and the Twelve had come into Caesarea, Philippi and the Master had stopped under a tree to gather the disciples in a circle around him to ask them a question. "Who do men say that I am?" Jesus had asked. The Twelve had shuffled about in their footsteps—each conscious of his doubts and his own fear to personally answer the Rabbi's question.

Chagrined, some had blurted out that the people said he was John the Baptist, or the Prophet Elijah, even Jeremiah. But Jesus had not been interested in what the people had to offer. He had spoken directly to the Twelve and asked them, "But who do you say that I am?"

It was at that moment that Peter had known the truth of the Nazarene. In the ignorant silence of the others, he had answered from his heart, "You are the Christ, the Son of the Living God."

The most beautiful smile had come across the Master's face. "Yes, Simon Bar-Jonah, blessed are you that this has been revealed to you from my Father in Heaven. And I say to you that you are Peter—Petros, the rock, and on this Rock, I shall build my Church and the Gates of Hades shall not prevail against it."

Tears of shame stung Peter's eyes as flies flew around his makeshift bed. How could Jesus build his Church upon a rock that had crumbled like the broken fragments of a rotted clay pot? He watched a fly land where his thumb still oozed his brownish blood. "Drink up, my little friend, and let the poison still your wings." He swallowed the moist earth in his breath and promised himself to rise after his rest and return to Jerusalem to be with the others. There was nothing he could do to make amends to his beloved Master, but he could at least face the Twelve in his shame and self-disgust. "At the very least, I can be a coward in the light of day."

ary heard John's voice calling out her name, but did not respond to his call. "Mary," the young disciple yelled out into the sunrise at Golgotha. "Mary, are you here?"

"Yes, John—over here," she finally croaked through

her parched throat. She rose to one elbow and swept aside the evidence of her despair which lay about her in the dust. Her body felt heavy, but she slowly rose to her full height and stepped away from the palm that hid her from John's view. She took the outer hem of her robe at her left shoulder and wiped away the soiled dirt that clung to her face. John took a long look at the Magdalene. Her long dark hair hung in clumps about her shoulders and her eyes were puffy and unfocused. Still, he made no comment as to her condition and waited for her to speak. "John, the Master is buried over there. Joseph of Arimathea, with help from Nicodemus, prepared his body with oils and laid him to rest in that tomb behind that rock." Mary's head bowed downward and she began to softly cry.

The disciple turned to look in the direction of Mary's pointed finger. Four Roman soldiers, three on high alert and one sitting to the side, stood guard about the edges of a large, round rock that had been rolled into the face of the cliff. The sitting one seemed to be applying a sign with a seal of some sort to the edges. John could see that the imprinted words were written in Caesar's Latin, which he neither spoke nor understood. The guards glanced up and observed them, but the woman and man posed no threat, so they did not seem to care and returned to their work. "Mary, let's go home," he said. Mary was either too tired or distraught to notice the soldiers, so John made no mention of the four. "Everyone is waiting for you in the upper room. Let us go and eat something—you look so hungry. Come, let's go to the others."

Mary stood as still as the statues that adorned the front of Herod's palace in Jerusalem. At last, she looked up at John and spoke with a sharpened tone, "I am not leaving the Rabbi. I do not care if I shall ever eat again!" John took a step toward Mary, but she stepped away from him and turned her back as if to run away. "Go away!" she cried, "Let me die with him here, John. Please, go back to the others and leave me alone."

But John went to her nonetheless. He took her into his arms and soothed the cries that racked her chest with a rolling grief. They stood in that position for some time until her tortured heaving settled into short bursts of sorrowful breaths. Finally, her stubbornness broke into a defenseless whimper that haunted the young disciple. True pain, unadorned and expressed in tiny, random shrieks that cut the desert air into shreds of despair. When the time seemed right, he led her away from the palms and down the road back to Jerusalem. The sun had risen over the desert cliffs, so they would need to walk quickly and look no one in the face. John took a furtive look over his shoulder at the guards as they were leaving. Now, two of them were standing on either side of the round rock and the seal was finished and in place. The other two would relieve them and alternate watches every third hour. "I will tell Peter of this when I see him later today—if Peter comes home."

Saul of Tarsus stood before the great door that led into the resplendent home of Annas. He reached for the heavy doorknocker—an intricate ram gilded in gold—and announced his arrival. He waited patiently, in the cool evening breeze that calmed the anxious Jerusalem, as the Israelites continued to celebrate the Passover in homes and tents across the city. "Imagine," he thought to himself, "one day ago I was sitting contently while listening to my teacher, Gamaliel, and now I am preparing to share this holy meal of remembrance with the family of the High Priest of Jerusalem and his powerful father-in-law." He straightened the embroidered front of his best robe and patted down his untamed red hair beneath the edges of his skullcap. A servant opened the door and wordlessly beckoned Saul to follow him. They traversed down a great hall where the trappings of immense wealth were displayed in every nook of the home. There were paintings, statues, carvings, and magnificent rugs. They arrived at a double set of gold painted doors, and the servant opened them simultaneously with an exaggerated flourish. Saul took a deep breath and then stepped confidently into the room.

"Ah, Saul of Tarsus," exclaimed Caiaphas, while rising from behind an intricately carved table covered with an elaborately sewn, silk table cloth, "how good of you to join us this evening—the meal that celebrates our people's release from the bondage under the Pharaoh." The High Priest strode over to the young Pharisee and greeted him with personal affection. He led Saul to the head of the table, where the imposing Annas was seated. "Father," Caiaphas said, "may I introduce you to Saul of Tarsus, the finest student of Rabbi Gamaliel."

The aging patriarch did not rise to greet their visitor, but smiled deeply and nodded his head. "Oh, yes," Annas said with a baritone voice that belied his aged face. "I know very well who this young man is, and I welcome him to our Seder on the second night of Passover. Please, sit down here, right next to me." He clapped once and the servants sprang to attention and brought an enormous cask of wine to the table. They filled the gilded goblet of each guest before Annas spoke again. Annas rose to his full height and surveyed his precious family that encircled the Seder table with great pride. Two nephews had joined them from afar on that day, and so they would celebrate the Seder again on that evening. He lifted his goblet of wine to bless the meal and to commence the ceremonial dinner and asked that all present wash their hands in a bowl of steaming water that was brought into the room for the occasion. Saul looked down upon the table as the old man prayed the blessing. Each of the symbolic foods was beautifully displayed on opulent plates and ample serving platters. There were eggs, hard-boiled—a symbol of their people's slavery and oppression in Egypt. An egg, when boiled, becomes hard like the Israelites. Only a people hardened by their slavery, and beholden to their God, could have the survived the long years that they roamed in the desert. There were the bitter herbs that reminded them of their former servitude, and the salt water to represent the tears that their people had cried as slaves. Also on the table was a roasted shank bone of lamb that symbolized that blood had been shed to bring them their freedom. A mound of haroset sat in the middle—a mixture of wine, nuts, cinnamon and apples, in remembrance of the mortar used to build the Pharaoh's treasured cities. Saul knew, from his studies, that the haroset was symbolic of their ancestor's triumph over the bitterness of slavery and their imperishable desire for freedom. There was the matzah, the unleavened bread that reminded them of the haste in which they had left Egypt. And, of course, the green parsley and celery, to remind them of the hope that comes with the advent of every spring.

When all the stories were told, the songs were sung, and a final blessing was said over the ingested meal as the children skipped away from the table in delight, Annas motioned for Caiaphas to join him at the head of the table. Now, only the three men remained, and Annas replenished their goblets to the brim with fine wine. The servants, sensing Annas' wish for privacy, took their leave and closed the entrance door to seal the room. The old man placed his right hand upon Saul's left hand that lay upon the table. And with his left hand, he reached for his son-in-laws right hand and held tightly to both of them. "My sons, the stories we have told tonight are the lifeblood of our people," he began. "It is our story, our customs and obedience to our Law that has brought us to this evening."

Caiaphas withdrew his captured hand and reached to drink deeply from his finely jeweled goblet. "Yes, Father, this is so," the High Priest said, "and our deep respect for the Law is why we found this Jesus of Nazareth guilty of blasphemy yesterday morning." His chest drew up in absolute authority and he continued with emotion, "No one man can claim to be the Son of God for then he is claiming to be our Holy God! My heart beats with contentment to know that this dangerous fool lies rotting in his tomb."

Annas nodded in agreement and turned to speak to the young Pharisee. "I understand that your visit to see our Governor Pilate was agreeable, my son," Annas said in response. "May I assume that the Nazarene's tomb is guarded from those who might wish to disturb it for personal gain?"

"Yes, my Lord," said the animated young guest. "I saw four Roman soldiers standing in place at the entrance just before arriving here for this wonderful meal." He began to thank his hosts; but Caiaphas motioned for him to continue with his report. "I chose not to speak to the guards, but did come close enough to read the Governors' proclamation imprinted in the wax on either side of the entrance. There is a rope cord that runs between the two seals, across the face of the round rock. Believe me, no-one can enter that tomb without killing the guards and breaking the seals," said Saul, who hesitated for a moment to add gravity to his next words. "I read the Governor's proclamation with my own eyes. The warning is quite clear—the penalty is death for those who would unhook the rope cord and attempt to roll the rock away from the entrance!"

"Thanks be to God," exclaimed a contented Annas. A deep laugh aided by the wine shook his ample frame. "Perhaps we should consider doing more with our friends, the Romans," he said in his mirth. "Pilate cannot afford another uprising or Emperor Titus will have his head delivered on a platter to Rome."

And with that said, the three men settled back into their chairs to enjoy the finest wine that would be served that evening in all of Jerusalem. Their plans had been executed to perfection, and the revolutionary teachings of the itinerant Rabbi would soon be washed away like the city's dust in the April rains. Without their Master performing tricks and signs that enthralled the masses, the Galileans would soon return to their homeland. If they insisted upon staying and causing trouble in Jerusalem, then Saul would hunt them down; and Annas and Caiaphas would use their considerable influence in the Sanhedrin Council, and even in Pilate's court, to squash these scruffy rebels without a trace of sympathy for their cause. The morning would bring new duties at the Temple, to administrate during the coming days of the celebration. But in the darkness of that evening, with their souls restored by the Seder meal and the remembrance of the bravery of their ancestors, they settled back into Annas' plush chairs in a delighted complacency, and drank with the happiness of free men. The wine would flow until midnight, until each would retire to his own bedroom chambers; confident that the problems that had arisen with the appearance of Jesus of Nazareth were settled. All was well—their power intact, the people happy in their ignorance, and the Temple Priest's coffers full of spring lambs and delicious wine. The Law of Abraham and Moses, as always, would prevail. It was a night that they would sleep in the sweet peace of knowing that the rabble rousing Rabbi was now merely a problem of the past, a mere bug, squashed in the middle of the night.

In the upper room of Mark's family home, the table was prepared for a far less elaborate meal than had been celebrated in Annas' palatial home. The unleavened bread and cooked lamb lay on simple plates atop a wooden table in the shadow of a wooden cask of wine. There were seven women and four men in attendance; and all but three of them—Mark and his mother and father—were from Galilee. Mother Mary had spent the day in mourning for her son. But she was pleased to learn from Mary Magdalene that Jesus had been properly buried in a tomb owned by Joseph of

Arimathea. The Magdalene would lead them to the tomb when the Saturday Sabbath was completed in the light of the first day of the week. There was a great strength and fellowship among the women, and each lifted the other out of the deep pits of their respective depths of grief. Only two men, of the Twelve that had traveled with Jesus of Nazareth for the whole of his ministry, had returned to the upper room since their master's crucifixion— John and his brother, James. The two brothers were the first two disciples of the Nazarene, and had been followers of John the Baptist when Jesus had first approached them three years before. The Baptist had recognized Jesus as the One who was coming and knew that he must decrease for the Lamb of God to increase. During that fateful meeting, they had recognized something very special about the Rabbi, and had implored Simon, and his brother Andrew, to drop their fishing nets and go with them to follow the one the Baptist called the Lamb of God. Jesus had nicknamed them the Sons of Thunder and had prodded them about their impetuous natures and volatile tempers. Over time, John had been deeply influenced by the Master's calm and loving manner, and had noted that his temper diminished as his understanding of the Rabbi's teachings blossomed. James, though, had retained the fiery explosiveness of his youth, and it was his boisterous voice that spoke the blessing after they each had thoroughly cleaned themselves in a warm water basin that stood next to the uneven stone fireplace in the far corner of the room.

"Father," he began, "our Rabbi and Master, has been vilified, then murdered, and hung from a cross. We pray for Your guidance to help us through our grief just as You guided our ancestors out of bondage in Egypt. We ask that You watch over our brothers and sisters who are not with us tonight. Guide them back to this home where we may gain strength in our love for each other, and in the teachings of our Master." All in attendance lifted their cups of wine to seal the blessing into place. Mark's father refilled their cups from the cask, and was thanked by the men for his hospitality. Most of the work had been done on the Day of Preparation for the Passover, and he had worked alone, since the women had followed Jesus, on that day, to the place of his death.

John stood to pour a fresh goblet of wine for Mark's father when the familiar knock reverberated from the front door at the foot of the staircase. He did not hesitate, tearing immediately down the narrow staircase as the rest of them stood at the top of the stairs to listen. Even though the knock was recognized, they would have to make sure that the one at the door was not here to dispatch them to their Master's fate. "Who is it?" cried out John and held his breath to better hear the answer. The voice that answered was hardly recognizable. Still, even in its weakness, John could hear a remembered strength in the muted utterance that barely slid through the door. Peter! Their leader was alive and home! John quickly unlatched the door and thrust it open as the others poured down the stairs to greet him. But was it Peter? The man standing at the door was crumpled within himself, staring downwardly as if in prayer. His shoulders slumped in an air of resignation and his hair and beard were matted with wet clay. For just a moment, John was not completely sure. "Peter!" John exclaimed and stepped aside so that the others could descend into the main room. The room exploded with joyous tumult as everyone chattered their greetings at the same time. John reached out to Peter and led him into the room, where he was immediately surrounded by the others. Still, the burly disciple did not raise his head nor acknowledge his friends in any way. Instead, his head slumped downward until his chin rested soberly upon his thick chest.

Mary of Magdala was the first of the group to speak. "Simon Peter," she cried out in excitement, "we are so glad that you are home and safe."

James came down the steps carrying a basin of warm water,

and two of the women approached Peter to clean off the wet mud caked upon his face. "Oh, Peter," Mary continued, "what are we going to do? They have crucified our Master and now we are alone."

For the first time, Peter moved to look up at the others. With self-hatred flashing in his eyes, he sharply said, "And why would you ask me, Mary? I am the one who denied him—not once, but thrice—and then ran away to save my own worthless skin. I denied even knowing who he was and left him to be nailed upon a cross." He waited for the women to draw a water soaked rag across his face. There were tears streaming down his cleansed face when he continued, "I am not worthy to even breathe the air of this home. Still, I could not hide forever in my shame. I have come back to beg for your forgiveness; although I will never forgive myself for my cowardice—never!"

It was Mother Mary who answered his pleas in the deathly silence that followed his defeated proclamation. "My beautiful son," she said, "has gone to be with his Father in Heaven. Peter, I ask you, would he forgive you for your fears? You did not betray him—you only ran to save your own life—the very life that we all need; for you are our leader, now that my son is gone."

Still, Peter could only shake his head in hopeless shame. Again, a rolling sob overcame his body as he slid sideways in a slow fall to the floor. John and James lifted him up to place him in a chair that Mark had set before the downstairs fireplace. The women peppered him with whispered affections, but the kind words slid off his shoulders as easily as the escaping smoke rose upward from the charred coals of the tended fire. James implored him to seize his personal power, to remember that he was Peter, the indestructible one of the Twelve—the rock! And though he heard the tender words of the women, and tried to recall the courage that he had squandered in the last two days, Peter's head remained tilting downward towards the smoldering fire. He wished that the flames would leap up and consume him for what he had done in denying his Master.

John only listened. He stared searchingly at Peter's defeated face, illuminated in reflection by the flames, and thought of his Master's parables and teachings. Praying silently, he asked that God would give him the words to convince his leader that he could not afford to fall into a paralyzing pit of self disgust. They needed his leadership. They needed his fearlessness to plan their escape from the city and return to their homes, before they were captured and crucified like their Master. As the voices of the others ceased speaking, as the futility of their argument to Peter became evident, John received an answer to his prayers in his own voice. "Peter, my brother," John said, "you know very well that you have our forgiveness. We love you in your strengths, and even in your weaknesses. We love you because you have always loved us and served to lead us through many dark days." John knelt on one knee so that his words could travel upward to the sitting disciple. "Still, I understand that it will be hard for you to forgive yourself. After all, you are a leader of men of which much is expected. But, I ask you, how many times has our Holy God forgiven us, the people of Israel, and demanded only our obedience in return? Time and time again, we were given another chance at redemption. Do you place yourself higher than our Holy Lord?" John hesitated to gauge Peter's attention. With conviction, he continued, "and if the Master was sitting here among us today, he would certainly rebuke you, yes—but you know that he would forgive you as he has so often forgiven all of us in the past." He reached his hand out to touch Peter's right cheek and wiped away a falling tear with a sweeping thumb. It was very difficult to see their proud leader in such pain. Nonetheless, the young disciple gathered his courage and pressed on, "Did not Jesus teach us the very essence of forgiveness? You, yourself, asked him a telling question after he told us the parable of the sinning brother— 'Lord, how often shall my brother sin against me, and how many times must I forgive him? Up to seven times?' you had asked, as we all sat in anticipation for his answer. Do you remember asking him this question? Those were your very words, Peter."

For the first time since he had arrived in the home, Peter raised his head to look into John's eyes and softly said, "Yes, John, I remember."

"And do you remember his answer?" John decried. "Well, if not, then let me remind you. Jesus said not up to seven times but seventy times seven. Don't you understand, Peter—if the Master would forgive you your trespasses, then who are you to deny that forgiveness to yourself? This is the greatest strength. This is a lesson from our beloved teacher."

Peter could not hold back an almost imperceptible nodding of his head. He reached out to grasp John. He smiled shyly at the others and rose from the chair to embrace the young disciple. "Thank you, John," he replied. Then, he wiped away the remains of the moisture that still clung like morning dew to his cheeks and opened his arms to the others. They moved toward him and held each other tight in the midst of a fear that gripped them to the guts of their stomachs. But they drew strength from being together and in seeing their leader back among them. Peter was home! And in the morning, one of them would leave the house to listen to the talk on the streets; to see where they stood with the Sanhedrin authorities and the Romans. For all they knew, they were as wanted as their Master had been, and could soon share his same fate.

After their dinner was consumed, they sat in the near darkness of the upper room and asked each other questions to fill in the gaps of their last two days. The quizzical banter went back and forth until they cobbled together the story of all that had happened. Had not the Christ told them at their last supper together exactly what was going to happen; and had it not happened in just the way he had foretold? They wondered in their confusion—how could he have known that he would be betrayed, arrested and sentenced to die? And where were the others—the other nine disciples who they had lived with, like brothers, for three full years? And where was Judas Iscariot— the one who had betrayed Jesus? At long last, when their passionate conversation was stilled by a shared tiredness, they extinguished the candles that lit the upstairs quarters. Mark and his father and mother took their leave to go down the stairs to their bedrooms. The others remained in the upper room, lying quietly on their makeshift beds, and each in their silent prayers. Suddenly, Mary of Magdala pierced the quiet by saying, "I am going to the Master's tomb on Sunday at the first sight of light. Perhaps someone will help us roll away the rock so that we may anoint Jesus with more oils. Who will accompany me?" The other women agreed to go with her on Sunday. They would rise before dawn and walk together in the earliest light to the tomb. John knew that their journey was pointless—after all, he had seen the posted Roman guards at the entrance of the tomb. But who could tell the grieving women not to do what they felt was best? He would stay in the city and send Mark out into the streets to find out if they could move about without the threat of arrest. And in the corner of the room, in a big clump of blankets, Peter lay, finally sleeping for the first time in two days. His gentle snoring floated above them like lyre music into their ears. Their Master was dead and buried, but at least they were together and could pray to his Father in the safety of that home. Tomorrow, they would search for the other eight disciples and inquire as to the whereabouts of Judas. In the coming days, they would make their plans to return home to Galilee—back to their fishing nets, their wooden boats and the families that they had left behind, and to a life that they had given up to follow the Rabbi Jesus. Soon, when the eight days of Passover were completed, they would journey home. They had no other choice.

❦

The Magdalene stirred awake from a fitful sleep in the very early morning light of Sunday, the first day of the new week. She quietly made her way over to a window, which offered a view of the eastern sky. Three shades of the lightest pink, stacked on top of each other to herald the coming day—the sun was rising with a glory unsullied by what had previously occurred. Mary waited in the solitude until a thin, orange line broke vividly at the base of the eastern horizon. Then, she knelt down to gently rouse Aunt Mary and Salome. "Are you ready?" Mary whispered, "Let's go to him." The women nodded their assent and rose without speaking to slip into their black mourning robes and fasten their veils into place. Each of the three women had been with Jesus at the foot of the cross, and Mary Magdalene and Aunt Mary had stayed to witness the hurried preparation of Jesus for his burial by Joseph of Arimathea and Nicodemus. Today, they would bring more oils and spices, and take their time to prepare the body with a woman's knowing attention. They had not been able to save his life, but they could certainly anoint him to show their respect and their love for their Master. With soft footsteps, they gathered their oil and spices and placed them at the head of the stairs.

Aunt Mary spoke first. "Let Mother Mary sleep," she said, "she can come with us tomorrow." The small sleeping form of Jesus' mother lay demurely at rest. Without awakening the others, they secured their wares and descended the staircase to leave by the side door. They were safe in the light—three women in mourning on their way to tend to a recently departed loved one. After all, a bereaved family would often offer their lamentations for up to thirty days after a burial. They would not be suspicious to a Roman soldier's eye, nor would they attract the attention of spies searching for rebels and devotees of the

Rabbi Jesus on orders from the ruling Sanhedrin. Just wailing women, grieving for a lost one, dressed in mourning black.

The three women moved forward with serious intent, and walked north from the Upper City to the Northern Gate, the most direct path to Golgotha and Jesus. Just before their arrival at the Gate, they came upon a woman named Joanna who was the wife of Chuza, a steward for Herod Antipas. She was a trusted friend of the Galileans and had offered the Master and the Twelve supporters monies over the past year. Joanna, recognizing the women came up them and asked, "Mary, are you going to tend to the Master?"

"Yes, please come with us, Joanna. We are going to need some help to roll away the big rock that sits in front of the tomb. Perhaps, you know someone?" And so Joanna did, falling into the slow but steady pace of the three women as they soft stepped past the Roman sentries assigned to watch the Gate. As the women suspected, the sentries did not engage them—seeing just four women on their way to cry over their dead. Golgotha was full of entombed bodies with women wailing their mournful lamentations into the swirling, desert winds. The Magdalene led the women toward Golgotha with hand signals and a single-minded focus. They knew what they would find when they arrived at the tomb—a three day old corpse too quickly wrapped in funeral clothes at the back of a dark tomb. And they knew how they would treat the body of the Master upon arrival. Lovingly. Perfectly. They would anoint him in a manner that was worthy of his beautiful spirit. But not even one hundred steps past the gate, their concentration was broken by a strong tremor that rattled them and almost threw them to the ground—a rumbling in the distance that rolled through their feet and shook the Northern Gate like a chafe of wheat trembling in the storm.

"What was that?" said a frightened Salome, "Did you feel that shaking?"

The other three answered, "Yes!" and all at once they quickly moved closer together to take each other by the hands when another lesser tremor shook their pathway. Now they were truly frightened and nervously babbled in their fear. They looked to Joanna, since she was a resident of Jerusalem, but she returned their quizzical looks with upraised hands.

Mary Magdalene was just as fearful as Aunt Mary, Salome and Joanna, but spoke to them sharply, "It is of no importance. Come; let's hurry to the Master. A little shaking of the ground is not going to stop us!" She quickened her pace so that the other three thought more of keeping up to the Magdalene and less about the frightening tremors. Soon, they were at the foot of Joseph's garden, on a path that meandered across a small mound to the face of the rock cliff upon which Joseph had carved out a family tomb—the final resting place for their Master. Mary looked up to where she had spent the evening after the crucifixion, among the palms that grew above the tomb. She was seven paces in front of the others as she made the final turn when she cried out loudly, "Oh no, the rock has been rolled away!" The others came up behind her and confirmed that the rock was pushed to the side and that the dark tomb lay open to the desert air. They were stunned.

Mary immediately surmised that the body had been stolen. "What have they done to our Master?" she shrieked. The indignity of his stolen body was too much for her to accept— they had mocked him, beaten him and then crucified him. Now this! She had endured his pain as if it were her own in every step of his path to the cross. And now, the filthy thieves had denied him his anointing and his deserved rest by stealing his body. His grave had been defiled! A red flushed anger arose in her from her feet to her face like the burning of heated oil being poured upon her skin. She collapsed to the ground and thrust her hands scratching into the dirt before screaming out to the others, "I must go. I must go now and tell Peter."

Aunt Mary, Salome and Joanna were confused and fearful.

They were too bewildered to even respond to Mary, and just stood silently in place staring at the black hole that marked the entrance. Their fear multiplied as the Magdalene took off running back to Jerusalem to find Peter. Without a word to them, she disappeared beyond the mound, as she hurried alone back to Jerusalem.

After a moment to gather her wits, Aunt Mary stilled the younger two women and said to them, "Let's go inside and search for him. I cannot understand what has happened." She could see that Salome and Joanna were fearful of doing so, but the older woman swore their protection in a blurted prayer to the Almighty. "Come with me," she said to them with a stolen confidence. And so together, they stepped to the entrance and entered into the cold, dank air of the tomb. They held each other tightly by one hand as they inched forward into the tomb, by staying in touch with the stone wall that coated their free palm with a cool moisture. As they approached the empty platform, where they expected to see their Master in repose, they were surprised by two young men dressed in white robes that dazzled them with a bright illumination.

"Why are you looking for the living among the dead?" said the one who was seated at the head of the stone platform. The women shielded their eyes as the brilliant whiteness of the men's robes caused them to blink in protection. Salome thought that they were whiter than even the whitest snow. Their terror overtook them and they bowed down to the ground without responding to his question. "He is not here, but is risen!" he said forcefully. "Don't you remember how He spoke to you when you were still in Galilee, saying, 'The Son of Man must be delivered into the hands of sinful men, and be crucified, and the third day rise again.' Now, go quickly and tell the disciples that He is going before you into Galilee, and there you will see Him. Go now and bear witness to all that you have seen and heard." And at once, the women remembered the spoken words of the

Master. An understanding of what the Master had said seized them and wiped away their confusion like a cleansing rain. With their feet energized by an anxiety intermingling with joy, they rose up from the ground and left the tomb in the direction of the daylight that now poured into the entrance. Once outside, they moved quickly toward the Northern Gate, as they scurried to Mark's house to tell the others. They ran with the vitality of children as the words of the dazzling stranger burst in their chests. They ran home with the good news.

ary beat the familiar knock upon Mark's door with an anxious force. When no one answered, she pounded her hands into the wood so that it could be heard in the corners of the upper room. "Please, hurry." Mark's mother answered the door and greeted the Magdalene. "Where is Peter?" Mary asked without a moment of hesitation.

"He is upstairs by the fireplace. Some of the others have come home—Andrew, Phillip and Nathaniel are here now," said the old woman who took such good care of the Galileans. "Mark is out looking for the rest of the men," she said as an unhearing Mary bounded by her and climbed the stairway with two-step leaps.

When she burst into the room at the top of the stairs, she went directly to Peter, who was speaking in a circle to John, James, his brother Andrew, Phillip and Nathaniel. The men stopped their conversation at the sound of her commotion, and looked up at the panting Magdalene. "Mary," Peter said with solemnity, "Judas Iscariot is dead by his own hand."

"Oh, Peter," Mary cried out, ignoring Peter's declaration, "they have stolen the body of the Master."

With the news still hanging in the air, Peter stood immediately and issued a clear order. "John, come with me to the tomb. I want the rest of you to remain here until the others arrive. We will be back as quickly as we can." He looked at his brother, Andrew, who had begun to protest, but one glance silenced the younger man's concern.

"Mary, did you see the Roman guards?" asked John. "When we left yesterday morning, there were four of them standing guard, and the tomb was sealed. Did they break the seal?"

"I saw no one, John," she answered. "The heavy, round rock that sealed the entrance had been rolled away. I could see right into the tomb."

Peter asked her, "Did you see Jesus' body? Did you go inside the tomb?"

"No, Peter," Mary cried out, "but I am telling you. Someone has stolen the Master's body. Please go there now. Please!" She could see that her words alarmed all of the disciples by the stunned looks on their faces. They chattered in low voices among themselves speaking of devious plots and schemes.

John and Peter left in haste through the side door and climbed over the fence that held the lambs and chickens in their pens. They covered their faces by drawing the hood of their robes tightly to their cheeks, and broke into a full run. If they were to be captured by the Romans now, their captors would have to chase them down at top speed. John, younger, and more familiar with the safest and quickest path to Golgotha, ran ahead of the stout leader's stumbling strides. Mary of Magdala trailed behind them, already exhausted by her previous run to tell the disciples of the empty tomb. They did not run unnoticed. Unlike the women's quiet walk past the sentries at the Northern Gate, the sight of two men sprinting at full speed thorough the Gate attracted the sentry's attention. They observed that the two turned in the direction of Golgotha—the senior sentry noted that with some curiosity and ordered an underling to take the news to the Temple. They were under orders from their commander to report any unusual activity to the Pharisee Saul, a Roman Jew, who would be at the Temple.

John did not slow down for even a moment's rest until he stood directly in front of the entrance to the tomb. "Mary was right," thought John. The large, circular rock that had sealed the entrance had been rolled to the side. The seals were cracked, and the sash that connected both sides of the seal lay tattered and hanging from the coarse outer edge of the huge rock. He knelt down to peer into the tomb—he knew from his traditional upbringing that to enter the tomb would render him unclean. It couldn't be done, so he waited in that crouched position for the arrival of Peter. He would know what to do. Peter would make the necessary arrangements to properly enter the tomb. And then Peter came roaring over the top of the slight mound, and without a moment's hesitation, ran briskly past John and into the tomb. His black hair shone with sweat and his breathing was labored in short bursts.

"Come, John, right now," he yelled to the younger disciple as he passed him. The truth of Mary's witness would have to be verified with their own eyes. John let go of his fear and his natural observance of the Law to plunge himself into the darkness of the tomb behind the footsteps of the fearless Peter. Within seconds, their eyes adjusted to the dark, and they looked upon the slab in which they expected to see the Master's wrapped body laying in rest. The body of the Nazarene had vanished. And yet, there upon the smooth stone bier was laid his burial linens in perfect position. It was as if the Master had passed through the anointed cloths as a divine chrysalis—a butterfly leaving his cocoon in place. On the right side of the bier were the neatly folded face shroud and the linen tie that Joseph and Nicodemus had fastened about Jesus' jaw to keep the jaw from sagging. "What type of thief would take the time to neatly fold those items? And how could the thief steal the body without tearing the visible oil saturated binds that had wrapped the Rabbi from his feet to just under his crossed and bound arms?" they questioned among themselves. For a moment, both Peter and John just stood in shock of the discovery as these questions rolled about in their heads. The evidence was baffling, and they were mystified.

But then—John believed. He understood and truly believed. "Peter, the prophecies of the Master have come true," said a soft spoken John. "He has risen from his death just as he said he would do." Still, the strong fisherman who led the surviving Eleven remained speechless. He did not agree, nor disagree, but simply stared at the evidence that lay in clear sight before his quizzical eyes. His still laboring breaths broke the silence of the empty tomb with a reverberating sound that bounced from the ceiling to the floor before escaping out the open way. The black hairs at the top of his chest tumbled over the neckline of the robe as his chest expanded in order to breathe in the stank air. So John approached him and placed his hand upon the larger man's back. There was nothing to do but to return back to the upper room, at Mark's home, to tell the others. Mary's report would be witnessed—her description confirmed by their own attendance. "Let's go home, Peter, to tell the others," said John, "I tell you, the prophecies have been fulfilled!"

Peter shifted his gaze to look directly at John. He could see the belief coursing through the younger man—the belief in the Risen Christ as prophesied. He gathered his breath to say, "We will be blamed for this, John. We will be hunted down by the Romans and the Sanhedrin and stoned or crucified for stealing the Master's body. All of us must prepare to go to Galilee in the darkness of the night, if we are to survive another day." John started to protest, but Peter silenced him with one glare.

And so they walked back slowly to the house and took great precautions to remain unseen by altering their route home. They moved slowly and held tight to the walls of the crooked, narrow streets. Nonetheless, they had to pass through the Northern Gate on their return, where a certain young, red headed Pharisee, alerted by a Roman commander's messenger to the Temple, observed their quiet walk. When the two Galileans passed from his sight, Saul busied himself to walk in the direction of Golgotha to check on the Roman sentries who would be guarding the tomb. But first, his eyes sharply followed the path of the two men as they made their way slowly back in the direction of the Upper City. "Well, that was strange. What had caused the Galileans to come to the tomb in such haste—and to return to Jerusalem like thieves in the night?" he thought.

eaching the garden, the Magdalene call out, "Peter! John!" She approached the open tomb for the second time on that day. "Hello, are you here? Peter! John!" She scanned the length of the garden in search of the two disciples, her two friends. Seeing no one, she climbed to the top of the gentle mound near the tomb and cupped her hands above her eyes to protect them from the risen Eastern sun. Her eyes swept over the horizon in search of Peter and John. "Where were they? Had they found the Master's body?" thought the Magdalene, exhausted by her earlier sprint back to alert Peter and the men of her discovery. Heaviness pressed down upon her body as if the rock that once sealed the tomb had rolled upon her. She swirled around to look for her friends in every direction before realizing that she was alone; utterly, completely alone. Again, she was in despair at that very place, and now a deep sadness arose in her that clutched her stomach and bore sharp tears of frustration. Her legs trembled with weakness, so she slowly descended the mound to sit down upon a flat rock near the open entrance of the tomb. Once seated, she released the lump in her throat that blocked her airway, and hopelessly sobbed into her cupped hands.

Above her sobbing, she could hear a man speaking to her

from a few feet away. At first, the closeness of his voice startled her. She looked up through her tear soaked fingers to see a gardener exclaim, "Woman, why are you crying? Whom are you seeking?"

His calming voice did not scare her. "Perhaps he can help me find the Master's body? Perhaps he knows where it has been placed? He looks like a kind man who would help me," she thought to herself. She could see that he was a simple, working man, so she answered him in a brave voice, "Good Sir, have you seen the body of the man who was buried here? If you have carried him away, tell me where you have laid him, so that I may go to him to anoint his body." She looked up to the gardener to hear his answer. He was dressed in a simple robe with sandals and a brown beard that cascaded downward below his expressive eyes and smiling countenance. The sun shone strongly on her from just over his right shoulder.

The gardener said, "Miriam!"

A warm flush came over Mary as she heard the calling out of her formal name. In the time between two breaths, she recognized the gardener, and she saw him for who He was—now her throat filled with an unimaginable joy. "Rabboni!—Jesus!" she said, as she fell to His feet and began to kiss them and wash them with her tears. She held on to His feet with great tenacity. He had left her once, but He would never leave her again.

With urgency, the Risen Christ said unto her, "Do not cling to Me, for I have not yet ascended to My Father; but go quickly to My brethren and tell them that I am ascending to My Father and to your Father and to My God and to your God." Jesus smiled down at her as she disengaged and looked up at Him from bended knees. In the midst of that smile, Mary lost her fears, her despair, and the desire to cling to her living Master. He was alive! He had lived beyond the wrappings of His funeral linens, and on the other side of three days in the darkness of a cold tomb. She bowed to her Master in obedience and smiled back at Him. A full understanding filled her like a great feast. She truly, finally...understood. And, then, as quickly as He had appeared, He was gone.

oseph of Arimathea stood unbendingly before his peers in the Council of the Sanhedrin. He was a man of wealth and prestige in Jerusalem, and his demeanor portrayed his assurance. He held his hands in a prayerful form and rested his wrists upon the elegant robe that he wore to all Council meetings. Caiaphas, the High Priest, had requested his presence before the Council on that afternoon of the first day of the new week. It was apparent that the Sanhedrin was in an uproar over his decision to bury the body of Jesus of Nazareth just moments before the setting sun had announced the commencement of the Holy Week. The request to appear had been rather forthright—two members of the Temple Guard had accompanied Joseph on the walk from his lodgings in Jerusalem. An explanation would be required, and the High Priest wasted no time in making his feelings of the matter known to all in attendance. The seventy-one aristocratic members of the Sanhedrin Council sat in a semicircle of three terraced rows of twenty-three, with five more seated at the very apex of the highest curve. By arranging themselves in that pattern, the priests, elders and learned teachers of the Law—the supreme authority, in both religious instruction and crimes against the Law, for all of Judea—could see and hear each other, as well as the entreaties of all those brought before them for questioning. Two clerks sat unobtrusively at floor level to record the reasoning and decisions of the judges on either acquittal or condemnation of the accused.

On that morning, like all other mornings save the Sabbath

and certain holidays, the Sanhedrin had convened in The Hall of Hewn Stone; a building on the Temple grounds that had been constructed without the use of iron implements. This Council had the right to administer criminal law, to keep their own police force, and had the power given to it from the Roman Empire to decree the punishment for all those who broke the Law, except for those in which death was the sentence. When a case came before them, any member of the Council could express to the others that he knew of a tradition that spoke directly to the matter at hand. As such, a binding decree could be issued. If a tradition could not be found, then a conversation would commence, which generally concluded with a balloted vote. For death sentences, though, they would go before Procurator Pilate, who alone could issue a final order of execution as an appointed official of the Emperor of mighty Rome. Only one seat was empty; the one where Joseph traditionally sat as a respected member of the Council. "Joseph of Arimathea," blustered Caiaphas, "you have been called before this Council, and your peers, to explain why you requested the body for the burial of the Nazarene—the Galilean charlatan who was tried and convicted of blasphemy, and then rightly crucified by the Romans, with our assent. We know you, Joseph, as a good man, a wise man who lives in accordance with the Law of our ancestors, and one who gives generously to the poor and afflicted." Caiaphas took a breath to tap down his rising anger, but failing to do so, thundered, "What possible reason could you have had to bury this blasphemer in your own family tomb? Why did you not let his body be thrown into the common burial pit with the rest of those who break our Laws?"

Joseph withstood the angry questioning without even the slightest bowing of his head or averting of his eyes. He waited until the clamorous chatter of his fellow Council members diminished into a low, rumbling murmur before speaking. He noticed a frightened Nicodemus in attendance—there would be no need to bring up his name or his helping actions into the midst of that snarling inquisition. "Is it not written in our Law that we are to bury our dead in accordance with our customs and beliefs? Now, I am aware that Pontius Pilate said to us, 'I am innocent of the blood of this man.' The Governor washed his hands of any responsibility for the death of the Nazarene. You Caiaphas, and you Annas," he continued with a riveting look toward the High Priest's father-in-law, "assented to the crucifixion of the Rabbi Jesus. And by not speaking up with all my heart at his trial, so did I. So now, my priests, his blood is on our hands and on the hands of our children." He paused to scan his audience—all of the Council members now sat in rapt silence as they listened to his deliberative explanation. "It was the least I could do to properly bury him. After all, Caiaphas, he was a Jew, a teacher, a Rabbi. He was one of us."

Caiaphas exploded with an outraged vehemence without taking even a moment to measure his response. "He was NOT one of us! You will remember that it was decided by this very Council that the Rabbi was a dangerous blasphemer. And, as I said in the foolish man's trial, it was better for one man to die, rather than to inflame the Romans and threaten the very existence of our people!" The High Priest stomped his foot in frustration to put a physical exclamation to his bitter pleadings. "Joseph, I should think you should be more concerned with your own blood rather than the blood on our hands. What you have done, by burying the blasphemer, is against our Law—and now, this Council will decide your very own fate! You may face expulsion from our community—a shunning. I don't see how you will run such a lucrative business if our people are forbidden to even speak to you!"

"With all due respect, my good man," said Joseph in return, "I was merely fulfilling the obligations of our precious Law. It is written from the days of Moses that a hanged man must be buried before nightfall so as not to defile the land. Even the most scandalous, the lowest and most indecent of our people must be buried in accordance with the Law." The confident Joseph paused to deliver his most telling ascertaition by reminding the High Priest, and the Council, in an expansive voice, "For our God said by His prophet that vengeance is Mine, and He will repay."

The relative calm that permeated the room as Joseph spoke exploded into an undisciplined eruption of arguing voices in either support or accusation of Joseph. Still, one voice made its way through the tumultuous atmosphere to be heard above all others.

"Joseph, I will not be lectured by you as to the tenets of the Law. What you have done, by burying the blasphemer, is against our Law—and now, this Council will decide your very own fate!" said the furious High Priest. But just as Caiaphas had finished his diatribe against the respected gentleman from Arimathea, the doors to the Council Chambers were burst open by a disheveled Saul, who sought permission to approach the High Priest. Once granted, the diminutive Pharisee, with his long, red locks bouncing upon his shoulders, scurried through the center of the assemblage, and climbed up to whisper a few words into Caiaphas' ear.

The High Priest betrayed no emotion upon hearing the news—he merely turned and looked at Annas and then addressed the gathered Council. "Gentlemen, I must leave to attend to a pressing matter at this time. We will reconvene tomorrow to decide the fate of our friend Joseph." He motioned for Annas and Saul to follow him into his private chambers in the back of the Council Chambers. "Joseph, I must ask you to stay in Jerusalem until this Council determines your just punishment."

Joseph nodded his affirmation with respect. "I have come to Jerusalem to celebrate the Holy Days of Passover. If I am needed, I can be found in the Temple, praying to the Almighty.

The Word of the Living God will see us through these dark days, just as He has always done for the twelve tribes of Israel."

The three powerful men exited the Council Chambers and chose a path through the pilgrims praying amongst the Temple's hidden nooks and soaring splendor that took them to a private anteroom located at the end of the grand portico. It was in that very room that Saul had received his orders from the High Priest just two nights earlier. Caiaphas led the way, swimming his arms through those who blocked his path in an agitated and regal manner. Saul followed closely behind, occasionally breaking into a quicker step to keep up with the long striding High Priest. And, just behind them, was Annas, who walked with the experience of a man accustomed to dealing with problems of the most serious nature. He moved forward resolutely, with purpose. He would not cloud his mind with wasted emotions—he knew anger and a self afflicted anxiety to be the indisputable parents of indecision. Caiaphas quickly ushered them into the dark anteroom. With trembling hands, he put a wax candle up against the embers in the fireplace. The candle sparked to life. When the room was illuminated, he turned to Saul and asked him, "Please tell my father-in-law exactly what you said to me in the Council Chambers."

"The tomb that held Jesus of Nazareth is empty. The governor's seal was broken, and the rock was rolled away. I personally searched the tomb, and the body is gone, stolen!" said the young Pharisee.

"That is impossible," said an incredulous Caiaphas, "Were the Roman guards unable to withstand an attack?"

"We shall ask them ourselves," said Saul, "I have asked the commander and the two sentries to meet with us in Annas' courtyard when the sun sets this afternoon. Forgive my boldness for arranging this meeting at your home without your permission, but I assumed that you would want to speak to them personally." The younger man bowed respectfully to the attentive patriarch.

"Your assumption was correct," intoned Annas.

Caiaphas rubbed his hands together in deep thought. Nervousness settled in his stomach, infiltrating his thoughts and congesting his clarity. "Where was the body of the Nazarene? Had it been stolen by the Galileans? Had the news of his disappearance spread to the streets of Jerusalem?" But one thought, above all, left the safety of his throat as he spoke it out to the others. "Father, Saul, is it possible that all that this Jesus preached has come to pass? Could he be resurrected from the dead, the true Messiah?"

At that moment, Annas rose to his feet. "Do not be ridiculous, my son," he exclaimed, while resting his right hand on the shoulder of the Pharisee. "I am sure the body was stolen to incite the people. It is our responsibility to crush these Galileans, these coarse, ignorant peasants, before the people accept this nonsense and revolt against the Romans. An insurrection would be suicidal. We would be crushed by the Romans like we step upon the grapes of our vineyards!"

"Yes," Saul interjected, "the guards at the Northern Gate sent word to me in the Temple today, that they saw two of the Galileans' behaving strangely this morning. They ran through the gate with great haste in the direction of Golgotha, and then returned in stealth like thieves. When I heard this, I hurried out to check the tomb."

"You did well, my son," complimented Annas. "As always, we will root out those responsible for this travesty. Even at my age, I will throw the first rocks at their stonings with glee."

Caiaphas' nerves settled in the strength of his father-in-law's argument. Of course, the old man was right. As usual, Annas had not let his fears overtake his understanding. "Thank you, Father—your words return me to our task," said Caiaphas.

"Let us go to your courtyard now. I have some questions for those guards, and their commander. God help them if they do not have the answers!" He stretched to blow out the candle and opened the door to step into the expansive Temple. In every direction, pilgrims sang and worshiped joyously to the God of Abraham, of Isaac, and of Moses—the God that would see them through that insolent challenge to their authority—The God of Israel!

Peter sat cross-legged in the late afternoon shade of the olive tree. He had returned to his hiding spot after his three denials of Jesus, to plan an escape from Jerusalem to Galilee for the remaining ten disciples and the women and friends who accompanied them. Judas, the Betrayer, was dead by his own hand—that was just as well. Peter had been unable to properly plan their escape in the upper room while everyone was ecstatically listening to the spoken tales of Aunt Mary and Salome, John and Mary Magdalene. Peter and John had returned that morning from witnessing the empty tomb to an exultant group of believers who had hung on every word of the story told by Aunt Mary and Salome. They told of men in dazzling garments, speaking to them and admonishing them for seeking the living among the dead. And then, the Magdalene had climbed the stairs to tell them that Jesus was alive—breathing, walking, speaking. She had seen Him with her own eyes, had touched His warm skin and He had lovingly spoken to her, "Miriam!" She in turn had spoken His name, "Rabboni!" Everyone had insisted that she tell the story over and over again and they became even more enthralled with each telling.

Still, in the midst of the jubilation, Peter had kept his

composure and clarity closely at hand. As their leader, he could ill afford to let an unchecked happiness render him blind to the obstacles that still stood in their way to freedom. After all, the stories were being told by women, and a man was required to witness an event for validation. Questions arose in his mind, "Why had Jesus, if it was true, shown himself first to Mary, a woman? And who were the men in dazzling clothing? Why had neither John, nor himself, seen neither the Master nor the strange men, on their visit to the empty tomb?" Now Peter was well aware that the Romans would be incensed to learn that the body of Jesus of Nazareth was gone. He had not forgotten that the punishment for the breaking of a Roman Governor's Seal was death—immediate, tortuous death. The Romans would not believe in the resurrection of the Rabbi, and the fanciful tales told by the emotional women—no, they would accuse the Galileans of stealing the body and hiding it for their own devious purposes. Surely, the wrath of Rome would come upon them when Pilate was informed. They would be hunted down and tried quickly, before walking to their public execution—the only question that remained in Peter's mind was whether they would be hanged, like the Master, or stoned in advance by their own people for infuriating the mighty Romans? He reached up to twist an olive from a low hanging branch. How much easier it would be to be the fruit of a tree? Growing from seedling to a delicious fruit by adding juice and flavor in every day of one's life. It was such a simple path to a fulfilling ripeness, and then to be eaten, or made into olive oil to be served in bowls for the dipping of bread by the people. A sure life and death without the pangs of hunger and the hard boot of the Roman Empire always aimed and poised at the nape of his neck. He placed the ripe olive on the tip of his tongue, closed his eyes and let his thoughts fall solely upon savoring its flavor. "And what if it was true! What if Jesus of Nazareth had come back to life just as he had said he would do at our last supper together. Could I even face him through the putrid stink of my own cowardice? Did I not tell Jesus that I would die for him? But instead of dying, or having been proudly nailed next to my Master on my own cross in Golgotha, I ran away and hid like a child frightened by shadows. But what does this matter at this time. The most important thing I can do now is to come up with a scheme to escape the city before daybreak. It is too dangerous to stay here for the rest of the Holy Week. God will forgive us. I will lead everyone back to their homes in Galilee, and pray that the Romans will not send soldiers to round us up like desert snakes to be fed to the fire. If Jesus is truly resurrected and alive, then he can visit us in Galilee in the coming days. Tonight, I am their last hope for survival—they see me as their respected, stout leader; and yet, my outer skin has been as easy to penetrate as the thin, green shell that holds this olive's pulp inside it's circular grasp." He spit the spent pulp upon the ground.

A hushed rustling of the leaves behind his back summoned his attention. He prepared to turn around slowly, fully expecting to be staring into the stoic face of a Roman soldier bent on delivering him to Pilate. "So this was how it ends. Captured and marched back into the city gates, like a hunted jackal roped to carrying sticks." There was no need to fight or run away from his fate. Finally, his death was here.

"Peter," a voice called out to him as he turned to find the voice. "Peter," it cried out once more. And then Peter saw before him the Risen Christ, with visible wounds in his outstretched hands, and others in a jagged pattern across his forehead. Standing before him was the man he had followed and loved for three years; his Lord and Master, alive and breathing! His joy at seeing Him alive was tempered by a tremendous shame that swept through him like the desert sandstorms of his youth, stinging his eyes with tears.

Without seeing, he rose and moved toward his Master. The normally bombastic Peter found that he was unable to utter even a single word—silenced by his shame and humbled. For the longest time, he stood in front of the Risen Christ with his head bowed and eyes focused only on the round wounds that pierced the Master's feet. Jesus did not move. A thousand words poured through Peter's mind as he summoned the courage to speak. A thousand excuses, then explanations, then self recriminations, and then, finally, to the only two words that he could possible say. "I'm...sorry," Peter said in a shamefaced voice, as contrite sobs racked his burly frame and his tears fell out of his eyes in cascades. "My Lord...I am so sorry."

The Lord Jesus Christ smiled upon him. He allowed Peter to exhaust his shame and did not speak until Peter had sunk unto his knees. They waited like that until the wracking sobs subsided enough for the Lord to be heard. "Yes," said Jesus. Though only one word, it filled an entire language of understanding and heart felt love which poured over the shaken Peter. "Do not speak of this," the Risen Christ spoke into Peter's grateful eyes. He found it difficult to see Jesus through his tears, but the Master's voice traversed deeply into his pumping heart. He tried to rise up to stand next to Jesus, but his legs quivered without strength. Jesus knelt down to him so that His face was inches from Peter's tears. He softly said, "Stay in the city and return to be with the others—I shall come to them soon." And Peter did exactly as he was told.

y the time Caiaphas, Annas and Saul strode through the black iron entrance gate of Annas' courtyard, the Roman commander and the two guards who had been assigned to protect the tomb of the dead Nazarene, were already standing in place with one of the servants. Caiaphas wasted no time in commencing with their interrogation without even exchanging the barest of pleasantries. "How did this happen?

How could you have allowed the Galileans to steal the body of the Jesus of Nazareth?" he thundered. "Commander, I thought I made it quite clear to you that the disciples of this charlatan would attempt to do this. Did I not tell you that their last deception would be worse than the first committed by the blasphemous Rabbi!"

The Roman commander stepped forward to speak for the three. "Yes, Caiaphas, you were very clear in your warnings. I have spoken to my guards. They tell me that the ground rumbled loudly in the early morning and that they ran away in fear of being swallowed up by the earth. I promise you, that they will be disciplined in the most severe manner."

"I should hope so, sir," said the High Priest with a cutting disdain evident in his voice, "I should not have to remind you that the penalty for breaking a Roman Governor's seal is death. What do you think the proper penalty should be for these worthless donkeys who ran away from a little rock slide? And as for you, Commander, perhaps Governor Pilate should determine your fate, yes?"

The commander was struck silent by that threat. Before he could muster up the courage to respond, the sagacious Annas stepped into the breach to offer some remarks. "Gentlemen, let us not forget that we are all on the same side. That is, on the side of Rome, of laws and responsibility toward her subjects." He motioned for them all to come closer so that he could speak without fear of being heard by the servants or others wandering on the street side of his garden walls. "If Pilate finds out about this unfortunate theft, the penalty for you commander, and for your four skittish guards, will most certainly be death." The aged patriarch nodded in the direction of Saul who affirmed Annas' words with a one time nod of validation. "So, let me make a proposition. Let's agree that we will not tell Pilate of your failings," said Annas. The three Romans breathed a collective sigh of relief upon hearing these words. "Let's have you say that the disciples of this Jesus of Nazareth came in the middle of the night and overtook you before stealing the body. Yes—you were overwhelmed by a group of armed criminals intent on stealing the body for their own devious needs. Do you understand?" Annas paused to allow the Romans a moment to grasp the new story and then looked to his son-in-law and gently bowed. "Son, I should hope that our High Priest can part with some of our Temple monies to help you spread this version of what happened to all of Jerusalem?" Caiaphas looked at his father-in-law as if he had gone mad, but agreed wholeheartedly with the request. "And should this unfortunate event come to Pilate's ears, we will appease him and make you secure," the old man said with a smile, "for even the Governor is not adverse to accepting a few shiny coins in the interest of keeping the peace."

The commander stepped forward to confirm the offer. "Father, are you saying that you will let this matter fade away if we tell the story that the Galileans overwhelmed us and stole the body? And that you will pay us to tell this story to all of Jerusalem, and offer us protection from Pilate in the event he learns of the dereliction of our duties?"

"Yes, my son," said Annas. "We will pay you each ten pieces of silver from the Temple's treasury. Of course, this little understanding must remain our secret. Is that understood?"

The commander gathered his two men in a tight circle to discuss the proposition privately. Saul stepped away from the group so as to offer them the illusion of isolation. He could see that the Romans were stupefied by the generosity of the proposition. Instead of death, they were being offered a small fortune to authenticate a different version of what had happened that morning at the tomb of the controversial Nazarene. It was a fortune for their failure. Within seconds, the commander completed the discussion with his underlings and turned to address the two High Priests. "Sirs, we thank you for your gracious offer. On the heart of Tiberius, we pledge to you that we, and the other two, will tell this story to everyone we meet. We accept your conditions with gratitude."

Annas nodded his satisfaction and took a few steps to settle into a stone chair in the middle of his garden. He reached down to touch his fingers to a flowering plant that glistened with moisture. A fine dust from the yellowed center floated effortlessly to the ground. Seeing that, Caiaphas spoke, "We will send over the money by courier this evening. I trust, gentlemen, that you will be most convincing. If I hear otherwise, then I may be compelled to speak to our good friend Pilate." He glared at the Romans with baleful eyes as they scurried out of the garden to return to their barracks.

Saul spoke first upon the Roman's frenzied exit. "I believe that they understood your request, Annas. I am sure it is unpleasant to have to offer them money, but it may be silver well spent."

Annas whirled in the young scribe's direction with a swiftness that belied his advancing years. "I hope that you also understand our request to you. You are to hunt down these Galileans, and bring them before us for questioning at the proper time. Watch their actions, and when you see them challenging any aspect of our Law—pounce upon them and bring them immediately to Caiaphas and the Sanhedrin." The patriarch shook the yellow residue from his fingertips by clapping his hands together. "Saul, you do understand, I pray. You were not selected by the High Priest for your opinions as to the merit of our plans—no; you were handpicked to persecute these heathens to their death. Our way of life, and our positions at the Temple, will not be threatened by the mad ravings of an itinerant preacher and the ignorant schemes of the coarse fools who followed him!"

Saul was taken aback by the withering accuracy of Annas' words as he thought, "Perhaps I had mistaken my place with the High Priests—I had been brought into the inner circle to execute a specific task, nothing more. As a student of the revered Rabbi Gamaliel, they must know that I would never waver from doing all I could do to maintain the purity of the precious Law."

"I deeply understand, my lord," said the diminutive Pharisee, "I will personally commit to destroying this rebellious sect before a single one of their ideas escapes into the air of Jerusalem." He bade farewell to the two priests with a deep bow. "Rest assured, my lords, that I will be as relentless as the desert sun."

"Then God be with you," said a quiet Annas, with his hand placed protectively at the peak of Caiaphas' spine. "Our fate may well rest in your hands."

arkness finally came to Sunday evening as Mary Magdala was at last able to take a refreshing drink of water to soothe her parched throat. She had recounted the story of seeing the Risen Christ so many times, over the course of the day, that her voice had weakened to a whisper.

"Again!" Her friends had begged over and over, "Tell us, one more time, exactly what happened."

"Please Mary, what did He say to you?"

"Were His wounds visible?"

"Was He angry and preparing for revenge?"

"Mary, are you sure you saw the Master and not a ghost or a vision?"

And Mary had answered each of their anxious queries with a patient retelling of the story that began when she heard His voice call out her name. "Miriam."

"Yes, Rabboni." —Turning to speak to a gardener, but recognizing the Master—falling upon the ground and reaching out to hold Him—His gentle admonition to cling not to Him so that He could ascend to God his Father at the appointed time. And of the sheer peace that flooded her with joy to see

Him alive again.

Despite the euphoria that surged with each telling, a dispirited heaviness still gripped the upper room like a slave walking slowly in his master's irons. The ten disciples present, heard her story, but did not understand. Their fear at seeing Jesus led away from them to his death had not lessened because of Mary's words. They knew her brilliance, but she was still a woman, and likely prone to letting her imagination get the best of her—hysterical. Surely, her story had brought them some respite from the constant gloom that permeated their hiding place, and for that, they were thankful. Mary placed her cup in place next to the vat that held their drinking water. "I don't think that they truly believe what I am saying. I think they feel that I am speaking of a dream, a wish that has come true in my imagination." Nonetheless, she did not feel the need to convince them that her witness was not imagined. She had known that Jesus had walked beyond His death at the very second that He had called out her name.

John motioned for her to join him by the same east window where she had witnessed that day's dawn. He pulled a wooden bench to a position just under the sill and prepared her seat by flicking the loose sand away with the back of his hands. Once Mary was seated, John retrieved her cup and filled it with more water. He sidled close to her so that their conversation could be heard above the tumult of the squabbling disciples. "Mary, I know what you are saying is true. I saw the Master's burial rags when Peter and I ran to the empty tomb this morning. He had passed through them without a single tear. Our day of glory is near!" he said in an excited whisper, while brushing her long hair aside so that her right ear lay open to his words.

Mary was happy to see that John believed. She asked the sinewy fisherman, "John, where is Peter? I saw him get up to leave this afternoon without saying a word."

"I am not worried about Peter—I would think he is preparing for our day of victory tomorrow, when the Messiah assumes his throne," said the young disciple. "Mary, we are going to be sitting in the Royal Court of the King of the World. Even the Romans will be our slaves!" John let his head roll back and laughed and shook his finger in the air. "I cannot wait to tell Pilate to fetch some water from the cistern for me—and he had better do it quickly."

"I don't think so," said the Magdalene while allowing herself a muffled laugh over John's enthusiastic description of the despised Roman Governor's trip to the cistern. "You have always thought that Jesus came to us to take over this world. No, my friend, He is showing us the way to another Kingdom—the Kingdom of God."

"But, Mary, He has overcome death. If your story from this morning is true, then He cannot be stopped. The true Messiah has finally arrived to free the tribes of Israel from bondage forever. Can you not understand—I will be sitting to the right hand of the King?" John's chest swelled with a shared pride.

But Mary gently shook her head to disagree. "John, do you remember what the Master said at the very beginning? Do you remember when He sat down on that mountain that looked over the Sea of Galilee and spoke to the multitudes?" said Mary. "The first time—just after you joined Him, with your brother James, and Peter and Andrew. I did not know you for another year."

"Of course, I do, Mary," said John.

"Thomas has taught me the blessings from that day—every single word that was spoken by our seated Master. I did not always understand them, until today," Mary whispered to John. "But this morning, when I saw Him in His risen glory, alive and breathing—now I understand what He has endeavored to teach us." John was quick to respond to her but Mary stopped him by placing a hand to his lips. "Listen to me, John, while I say what He said on that mountain. Please listen to me so that we can teach our people these words when the Master goes to His Father as He told me today." The young woman cleared her throat and placed her mouth within a finger's touch of John's right ear. When he was settled, she began. "'Blessed are the poor in spirit, for theirs is the Kingdom of Heaven. Blessed are those who mourn, for they shall be comforted. Blessed are the meek, for they shall inherit the earth. Blessed are those who hunger and thirst for righteousness, for they shall be filled. Blessed are the merciful, for they shall obtain mercy. Blessed are the pure in heart, for they shall see God. Blessed are the peacemakers, for they shall be called sons of God. Blessed are those who are persecuted for righteousness' sake, for theirs is the Kingdom of Heaven.'The Kingdom of Heaven, John," said the Magdalene as she turned his face to see her. "He came to tell us to repent of our sins and seek the Kingdom of God."

The disciple opened his eyes to her and thought, "She has been changed today by what she has seen. I am looking at a woman who is no longer seized by seven demons but seized by the spirit of the Risen Lord—a true follower of the One." He smiled at the Magdalene and took her hands in between both of his. "I do remember, Mary, I remember everything the Master said that day to the crowd. It was the day we knew that we were with the long awaited Messiah, although we had already seen Him heal the sick and afflicted throughout all of Galilee and most of Syria. It was the day that He first spoke to us about who He truly was."

Their conversation was interrupted by the heavy footsteps of a man ascending the stairs. They both flinched without thinking, but were relieved to see the familiar form of Peter at the head of the stairs. The leader strode quickly to where they were seated and wasted no time in asking a question. "John, how many of the Eleven are here? Has Mark found the rest of our brothers?"

"We have everyone here in this room except for Thomas. Mark has heard that he was at the Temple today, but did not find him yet. The rest are arguing happily, Peter, after hearing Mary's story of seeing the Master this morning, alive and well," said the contented John.

"Good. Now listen to me carefully—No one, save Mark, is to leave the upper room until I give further notice. Is that understood?" said Peter in an imperious tone.

"But, Peter, tomorrow is our day of glory—the day our people have sought for generations. You cannot be serious about asking us to stay hiding like house mice up in this room while our Master ascends to His rightful throne." The larger man's response was quick and vicious.

Mary moved quickly away from the two of them to her resting place as Peter unleashed a torrent of oaths that ricocheted amongst the wooden beams of the vaulted ceiling. "I do not seek your opinion," he snarled, "simply do as I say or I will strike you to the ground without mercy. No one, save Mark, will leave this home, unless they do so by stepping over my dead body. Is…that…clear?" He glared at the younger disciple with the bloodthirsty eyes of a rampaging soldier.

John had seen him like that before and knew that a continuation of the argument would be futile, and perhaps even dangerous. He thought, "I should remind him that we are disciples of Jesus and there is no need for such bullying or spoken oaths. No, that is a battle for another day." John answered instead, "Yes, Peter."

"Fine, and instruct Mark to find Thomas in the morning. I want all of us here—safe and together," said Peter. "Now, I would like to speak with everyone at the main table in a few minutes. Will you ask the women to prepare us some food and wine? I will join everyone as soon as I shake the dust from my beard."

John agreed quickly. "I will gather all of them. Mark's father bought us some fish this morning at the market and we still have some of the wine that was brought to us by Joanna. We will wait for you at the table."

But John did not wait without emotion. Mary's spoken recital of the Rabbi's blessings on the mountain reverberated in his head as he strode into the midst of the Galileans to deliver Peter's request. "Were these blessings the key to understanding the Master's true heart and purpose? Still, Mary is a woman, hidden from the ugliness of a man's life. This is still a hard world, and the sword is the equalizer of last resort!" he thought. Images filled with the pageantry of the glory that would surely be coming in the morrow paraded before his eyes. Tomorrow—the day that the true Messiah would finally reign as the prophets had foreseen. "Peter will soften when he hears the trumpets calling."

eter assumed his place at the head of the wooden table that stood solidly in the center of the upper room. To his left sat the brothers, John and James, whom the Master had called the Sons of Thunder, from Zebedee. The fiercely ardent siblings had been followers of the Baptist, and had witnessed the baptism of Jesus of Nazareth by the wild eyed and bedraggled desert prophet who had foreseen the coming of the Christ, the lamb of God. To his right sat his own brother, Andrew, who had first brought Peter to meet the strange Rabbi who spoke in parables and healed with a wave of his faithful hand. To the right of his brother was Matthew, the former tax collector, a notorious sinner who had been absolved of his treachery in his devotion to the Lord. He was joined at the table by Phillip and Simon the Zealot, the disciple who had been witness to one of the Master's first miracles—the changing of water into wine at a wedding three years previous in Cana. To the left of James and John, sat the other three—James the Less, Bartholomew, and Thaddeus. Ten in total, for Thomas had not been found, and Judas Iscariot's rotting corpse was still mangled on the large rocks just below the hanging tree, with the broken rope still tight around his neck. Let the crows ravage his skin into a thousand pieces, and sharpen their beaks upon his betraying bones for the rest of time. Traitor! And standing behind the seated ten, were Mark and his mother and father, Mary of Magdala, Jesus' Mother Mary, Salome, and Aunt Mary, the wife of Cleopas, who had left in the morning to return to Emmaus in Galilee with a fellow pilgrim. Aunt Mary had stayed behind to care for Mother Mary in her grief. The imposing leader of these Galileans surveyed the room before speaking. Around the wooden table sat the most ordinary of men, who had been chosen by the Nazarene to give up their lives to follow Him. It had begun when He asked the first four to leave their fishing boats anchored to the shore. They had done so. They had walked away from their livelihoods and away from their wives and families to spend the next three years walking through all of Galilee and Judea with their chaste teacher. They wondered if their boats were still navigable or covered with barnacles and the green rot that destroys the wooden hulls of abandoned boats. They were ordinary workingmen, neither educated in the Scriptures nor the cultural arts, nor unable to speak even a word of the Greek language that married the writings and ideas of the formally educated. Peter thought, "And I see that they are still sitting here in their fear—just as I would be if the Lord had not appeared to me this very afternoon to restore me, despite the evidence of my cowardice."

"Women, thank you for this fish and bread that you have prepared for us," the demonstrative Peter began. "We are always grateful that you watch out for us and feed us when we are hungry, and offer us drink when we thirst."

The Magdalene answered for the women. "It must be so or the lot of you would starve like jackals without water in the desert. You men love your words more than your stomachs," she said in a loving yet slightly reproachful tone.

Peter laughed, but quickly turned his attention to the matter at hand. He knew that the Galileans would take their lead from him—if he showed fear, they would tremble accordingly; and if he showed faith, then their own beliefs would be strengthened. "My friends, I have made my decision. We will not travel back to Galilee under the cover of this evening's darkness," he said, "but remain in Jerusalem until the Holy Days are over. I must ask each of you, except for Mark, to stay in this upper room—I am certain that the Romans, and Caiaphas' spies, will be searching for us as the accused thieves of the Master's body. We will be safe here if we do not challenge that story."

Matthew, the former tax collector, spoke the thought that was on the lips of the other eight disciples. "Peter, do you believe that the Lord Jesus has risen from his death. Could it possibly be true?"

The seated disciples erupted with shouts of their own, so Peter took the time to carefully consider his answer amidst the excited chatter. He wondered, "Should I tell them that He came to me this afternoon—that He is as alive as when we were all last together at this very table? No, the Risen Christ obligated me to say nothing of this; and I do not intend to ever fall short of His wishes again. Not ever again!" Peter tore a piece of bread to dip into the oils that bubbled around the steaming fish. The others watched as the black bearded one considered Matthew's question while chewing on the drenched bread. He drank deeply from his wine filled cup before responding. "All will become known in time, my friends. There are prophecies coming true that are beyond our understandings. Do not be gripped by your fear, though—now is our time to pray to the God of Israel in the name of His son, Jesus, to protect us from our enemies. Our God will watch over us," said Peter. "Mark, I want you to go tomorrow and find Thomas—we all must be here in the upper room, together and safe."

Mark stepped forward from his place on the wall, standing next to his father and mother. He was proud that his father had offered his home to the Galileans for their lodgings during the Holy Week. Peter was right, they would be safe here for Mark's father was a respected merchant, and neither the Romans, nor Caiaphas' lackeys, would raid their home unless provoked. It was a clever plan to allow the authorities to put forth an unchallenged story on the disappearance of the Master's body. As long as the Galileans did not openly contradict their story in the streets of Jerusalem, they would probably be left alone. "I will do as you wish, Peter," said Mark. As he spoke, there was the familiar knock at the door at the base of the stairs. "Perhaps that is Thomas coming home now," said the young and trusted friend of the Galileans and he quickly descended the stairs to find out if indeed that was so.

"John, and you too, Mary...the time has come for us to begin to build the Church of the Nazarene," said the thickset leader with authority. "There are others that may join us soon. Will you plan a way for us to worship in the safety of this home? Just follow the words of our Rabbi."

Peter rose to his feet and thundered while bringing both of his fists crashing to the table, "If we cannot go to the Temple for the rest of this Holy Week, then we will bring the Temple inside these very walls!" The disciples roared their acclamation, delighting in the show of confidence from their chosen leader. The Peter that they knew had returned—as bold and fearless as they had always known him to be—Simon the rock.

In the tumult, John looked over his left shoulder to where the Magdalene stood erectly against the wall. She nodded to him as if she had somehow expected that request from Peter. He thought, "This is not the same woman who I brought home from Golgotha on the morning after the crucifixion." John turned and said to Peter, "It shall be done," but no one heard him voice his compliance in the commotion.

At once, Cleopas appeared at the doorway with Mark in tow, and a man not recognized by the Galileans. Cleopas ambled over to his wife, Aunt Mary, and whispered something privately into her ear. The brother-in-law of Mother Mary's husband, Joseph, then bent down to speak tenderly to his sister-in-law, who touched her right hand upon the sagging jowls of the dusty pilgrim. Peter held up his hands to quiet the disciples. "Cleopas, I thought you were going home to Emmaus. What brings you back among us?" asked Peter.

The portly Galilean looked out upon the youthful faces that awaited his answer. These were hard men who had traveled with the Master for three years, often journeying for days without food or wine. They had walked with nothing but their robes and sandals worn thin by the cragged rocks of the region. Cleopas had known some of them as children, but he could no longer find the innocence that had once lit their faces with such promise. The eyes that were fixed upon him now were of lonely men—abandoned, fearful, and confused. He delighted in knowing that the story that he was about to tell them might feed their very souls. "I have something to tell you all," said Cleopas as John handed him a goblet brimming with Joanna's wine. "My friend and I were walking back to Emmaus in the midday when we were beset upon by a stranger who asked to join our conversation. I believe we first saw him just a few minutes walk from Bethany—yes, it was right about there, wasn't it?" he inquired to his fellow pilgrim.

"Cleopas, you old goat," Peter exclaimed impatiently, "go on—we haven't all day to listen to every step of your journey. Who was this stranger?"

"Oh yes, of course," replied Cleopas. He gathered his breath to continue, "there was this stranger who came up to us from behind and called out. 'What kind of conversation is this,' the tall stranger had asked, 'that you have with one another as you walk and are sad?' Well, I took a long look at the man, but did not recognize him—although I could see that he spoke like a Galilean. So I told him, 'Good sir, we are returning home from Jerusalem where we went to greet the Messiah, but he was captured and murdered by the Romans. Do you not know what has happened in Jerusalem? There is nothing for us here now, so we are returning to our homes and livelihoods.'" Cleopas drank deeply from his goblet and went on with the telling. "The stranger asked us if we were true believers in Jesus of Nazareth. 'Do you believe the prophets who prophesied that the Messiah would rise from his death on the third day? Speak now, have you heard that the tomb was found empty this morning in Golgotha?' he questioned us in great seriousness. Now, I must tell you all the truth. I heard the stories of what happened at the Master's tomb this morning, from my wife and the Magdalene. Women, do not judge me harshly, but I thought that you were speaking of visions that you wished into existence. So I told the stranger that I had heard stories this morning of an empty tomb, but I believed them to be, well—just stories," he said sheepishly while looking over to his wife. A potbellied laugh tremored through his pudgy frame as Cleopas weathered the stern look on Aunt Mary's face. "And no sooner had I said this, then we were rebuked by the stranger," Cleopas said, "as he spoke in great detail as to the prophecies regarding the Messiah. 'O foolish ones, he told us, you are slow of heart to believe in all that the prophets have spoken! Ought not the Christ to have suffered these things to enter into His Glory?' It was as if we were walking with Rabbi Gamaliel, himself, so learned were his words."

Cleopas reached across the table for a piece of bread and fish to put upon his plate. Peter was a little quicker and moved the bread a finger's length out of the larger man's reach. "Finish this story, my friend, and you will eat like a king," Peter murmured below his breath.

"So be it—you will starve it out of me! At this time, my friend and I decided to stop in a traveler's inn to take a meal. The stranger was giving us such an education that I asked him if he would join us for dinner, even though I was certain he would continue to rebuke us for our lack of faith," said Cleopas. "He sat at a table with us, and I took the time to look carefully at his face, even though it was partially hidden by his cloak. I did not recognize him. But then, just as he broke the bread to serve it to us, a veil lifted from my very eyes. I could finally see who he was—Jesus of Nazareth, my nephew, the Messiah! And when I said so, He vanished. I tell you this on the blood of my children; we talked and broke bread with the Risen Christ!"

For just a moment, there was silence in the room. The respite was short-lived as James, the more demonstrative brother of John, leapt to his feet with a striking disbelief. "Please, stop all of this. Are we to believe that Jesus would appear first to a group of women and then to old Cleopas before he would come before his own disciples? We are the beloved ones of the Master—his own brethren. These stories are ridiculous and only serve to deepen the pain of losing our Master." All of the other disciples agreed with James except John, who believed, and Peter, who had already witnessed the Risen Christ in the olive grove.

A voice called out in the middle of the banter, soft in timbre, but strong enough to be heard. "Peace be with you." Everyone in the room turned to find the source of that voice. And there Jesus stood!—Breathing, smiling, and gazing upon them with loving eyes. But how had He entered the room? The doors had been locked, and they had heard neither the familiar knock nor the sounds of steps upon the stairs. He had simply appeared as if He had passed through the walls. The Galileans shook with terror—was the man who stood before them a ghost? So Jesus stepped into the midst of them and said, "Why are you troubled? And why do doubts arise in your hearts? Behold, my hands and my feet, that it is me. Come and handle me; a spirit does not have flesh and bones as you see I do." And so they surrounded Him and some were brave enough to touch His skin and wounds. "Have you any food here?" the Master asked; and it was given to Him, promptly, by the Magdalene. Everyone watched Him as He placed the fish on the tip of His tongue and began to chew. The disciples and the others could see that He was in His human form—not that much different from their last meal together, save the scars that bore the proof of His earthly suffering. Still, how had He entered the room without coming through the door?

An ecstatic joy battled with confusion, which gave way to an overwhelming sensation that struck them mute. They wanted so hard to believe in what they were seeing but they were dumbfounded and conflicted. Terrified by what it meant to see their Master alive again. Still shaking with fear, they sank slowly into their chairs, saying nothing as Jesus unhurriedly ate the fish and sighed contently over its flavor. "Peace to you. It was written that it was necessary for the Christ to suffer and to rise from the dead on the third day, and that the repentance and remission of sins should be preached in His name to all nations, beginning at Jerusalem. And you are witnesses of these things. Behold, I send the Promise of My Father upon you, but stay in the city of Jerusalem until you are given power from on high." And then He breathed a spirit onto them that released them from their fears and brought them to their destiny. It was the moment that sanctioned their selection of three years previous. There was a great whooshing that pushed the disciples back against their seats, as their hair quivered like river reeds in the wind.

Though now empowered by their Lord in word and wind, no one spoke a word till Jesus spoke again. "Receive the Holy Spirit. If you forgive the sins of any, they are forgiven then; if you retain the sins of any, they are retained." The disciples struggled to understand. Was the Master telling them to forgive those who had murdered Him? Was He empowering them to teach forgiveness to the people? They knew that only God could forgive sins. Was He telling them one could find the precious spirit of forgiveness if one found the Risen Christ?

In the end, the Galileans fell prostrate upon the ground and began to ardently pray. The women surrounded Mother Mary and shared their prayers in the joy of seeing her son alive again. The Lord Jesus Christ looked upon them before leaving them to their beseeching. The ten disciples, and the others, petitioned the Almighty God in a loud voice to unshackle them from their terror and to bring a new understanding into their hearts. Kneeling, they pounded their hands unto the stone floor and prayed with voices that surged together in community—one voice, one thought, one rock upon which all could be built. And try as they did to still their fears, they could not banish the one thought that dominated all others; the one thought that simply changed everything. The Christ has risen.

t was becoming increasingly clear to Saul that he would not be returning to his father's tent making business in Tarsus for quite some time. His life had been simple in Tarsus—the business supplied the Romans with the plentiful goat's hair cloth, cilicium, which was central to the weaving of tents, sails, and even some of the Roman's personal cloaks. These fine strands were perfectly suited to be woven into tight patterns that kept in the warmth and offered complete protection from the swirling desert sands that could shred lesser fabrics into frayed rags, flapping pitifully in the harsh winds. No, it would be a long time before he would kneel down to weave with his father, or enjoy his mother's delicious meals. Caiaphas and Annas had seen to that with their selection of him to monitor the situation with the dead Nazarene and the uneducated gang of filthy Galileans who had devoured his blasphemous words like sweetened figs. Saul sat by himself, as the second day of the week introduced its arrival in a flickering light. The food before him bore no resemblance to his mother's fine cuisine and his morning drink was tepid and tasteless. He thought of his father—so precise in his craft. "Tent making and sail making requires such an understanding of the way the strands were to be woven together. Actually, the way all things should be built and maintained. Done properly, and the owner would have a tent that could withstand a five day sandstorm in the open desert. A sail could ride the winds to the farthest Greek Islands that sparkled in the sunlight. There was a pattern that must be followed, and I am thankful that my father gave me this understanding. And I am just as thankful that he sent me to be educated at the feet of the revered Rabbi Gamaliel. It was in the Rabbi's spoken wisdom that I found the same principles upon which to build my life—just like those woven strands that give the tent its strength against the unpredictable winds, and the woven sails that would not shred even during the fiercest tempest." The young Pharisee cleansed his plate and threw away the last vestige of his tepid drink onto the inner courtyard of his lodgings. "Let the Earth taste that swill—even a desert cactus would deny this sustenance!"

He rose from his seat and decided to go the Temple to see his Rabbi that morning. If he arrived early enough, he could speak with the holy man after the Rabbi had completed his morning prayers, and before his students would gather reverently around his speaking perch in the Temple. He gathered his robe about him and strode into the streets with his bowlegged gait. Jerusalem was calm. So far, at least, the story of the stolen body of Jesus had not been embellished into a rebellious celebration. "I certainly hope that the people remain tranquil. The Romans treat celebrations in the exact manner that they deal with insurrections—with flashing swords dripping with the blood of the participants!"

Upon arriving at the Temple, Saul stood in place behind a kneeling Rabbi Gamaliel, as the aged teacher spoke his prayers into his open palms. No Rabbi in all of Jerusalem knew the Torah, the sacred texts of the books of Psalms and Proverbs, and the venerable words of the prophets Isaiah, Jeremiah and Ezekiel, more intimately. His scholarship was renown from the gleaming white buildings in Alexandria that reflected the blue waters of the Mediterranean, to the green foothills of India that climbed majestically to the top of the world.

Saul knelt down behind him to pray his own prayers, and was deep in his entreaties to God, when the Rabbi's blue-veined hand touched him gently about the shoulders. "Saul, my son, it is good to see you. You left so quickly the eve of the Sabbath when Caiaphas asked to speak with you."

"Yes, Rabbi," said the respectful scribe, "I wish to speak with you about his request. May I have a moment of your time?"

Rabbi Gamaliel wordlessly signaled his agreement and waved a dispatching hand to the first of the students who were now arriving to sit at his feet. "We can speak here; what is it, my son?"

Saul looked directly into the deep blue eyes of the cherished Rabbi. He had such wisdom, compassion, and understanding. The orbs twinkled with a certain beauty that can be seen only in the eyes of the contented, of those who live their peace. "Rabbi, I have been asked by Caiaphas, and his father-in-law to handle a matter of the utmost importance," said Saul. "They are very concerned with the Galileans who traveled with the crucified Nazarene. The High Priests fear that the death of their Master may inspire the Galileans to incite an insurrection among our people—you know how the Romans would respond to that."

"And what have they asked you to do, my son?" asked the Rabbi, with a surge of joy could only come from a proud teacher to his former student.

Saul took a step closer to the Rabbi to speak without concern of being overheard. "They have asked me to keep a close eye on the Galileans, and to bring them before the Sanhedrin if they continue to speak of their Master to the people. It will not be tolerated by the High Priest."

"Ah, I see," said the genial Rabbi as a sly smile creased his face, bringing tiny wrinkles to the corner of his eyes. "Are you in accordance with their request—do you believe them to be a genuine threat?"

"Rabbi Gamaliel, let me speak straight from my heart. I am not concerned about the ravings of these uneducated fools who were deceived by the magic tricks and clever parables of this Jesus of Nazareth," said the redheaded Pharisee before continuing, "No, I am angry—furious, if the truth be told. I am incensed at a man who dared to claim to be the Messiah of our people, but was not even strong enough to avoid his hanging like a common criminal. Rabbi, it would have been better had he been stoned or beheaded—no real Messiah would allow himself to be crucified, which defiles the very land that he hangs above!"

"Now, Saul, where did you learn this?" said the wizened Rabbi, as a mask of exasperation flushed upon his features.

"Why—from you, Rabbi. From sitting at your feet and learning about the One who would come as the King of Israel—the One who would lead us out of this despicable age and into the shining glory of a new era. You were very precise, my lord, in teaching us that a strict adherence to the Law was our people's only way to survive until the true Messiah would arrive," said a passionate Saul. "Obedience, discipline, and perseverance. You taught us what God said to Moses on that mountain in the exodus in the beginning. 'Obey My voice and keep My covenant and you shall be a special treasure to Me above all people.'"

"Ah yes, my son, but did I not also teach you tolerance and charity toward those who do not live their lives in strict accordance with the Law?" the Rabbi exclaimed. "Did I not teach you that our God is as loving as He is strict; as forgiving as He is vigorous in His judgments? Did God not also ask Moses on that same mountain to tell our forefathers to stay far away from false matters and to not kill the innocent or the righteous—to seek not to oppress strangers, since we know the heart of a stranger as we were once strangers ourselves in the land of Egypt?"

"But, Rabbi Gamaliel," Saul retorted, "please forgive my impudence in challenging your wisdom, but this Jesus claimed to be the Messiah. He said, 'I am the One.' To say that he is God's Chosen One, but to die powerless and nailed to a cross— is that not like saying that God himself is weak and powerless? This is utter blasphemy and I sing joyously to the heavens that Caiaphas and Annas chose me to destroy this claim so that it is never spoken of in the walls of this Holy City."

The respected Rabbi motioned for Saul to take a seat next to him where his students would soon gather in a semi-circle to hear his lessons. He waited patiently for the younger man's breathing to return to its normal cadence. He looked upon his finest student and felt a source of pride in seeing how much the young Pharisee loved, and was obedient to, the Law. And yet he saw darkness in Saul's soul, a murky place where his zeal was stronger than his heart. A black anger that was wide enough to cover all of the light. He reached out to hold Saul's hand and spoke quietly, but with all of the authority that the Rabbi could muster. "Be careful, my son, for your mission is driven by your hatred. We are men, and even the most obedient of us are still just men— flawed and always in need of God's guiding hand," whispered the wise Rabbi. "It is dangerous to judge others so harshly, simply because they stray from a full acceptance of your most cherished beliefs." Gamaliel summoned up the authority that he held in his reputation—built by the acknowledged discoveries of the true meanings that he had so often discerned from the sacred, ancient texts. He summoned up every single year of his wisdom, gained from careful study of the Torah, to speak a final lesson to his most conscientious student. "Let Almighty God be their judge, my son. The Lord will surely determine their fate." Gamaliel prayed in silent fervor that Saul of Tarsus would be wise enough to understand what the Rabbi had come to know in the course of his entire existence.

Saul looked up at his teacher and nodded his head to affirm his understanding. He kissed the revered rabbi upon his forehead and rose to take his leave. Bowing a good bye to his teacher, he said upon straightening, "Thank you, my Rabbi, I do understand. Our Almighty God will surely judge each of them, and even the Nazarene in his death; but I also understand what I have been called to do—to bring these blasphemers, these pretenders, to the place where they will face His wrath."

The Rabbi turned to greet his students. He motioned for them to sit around him and smiled at their eagerness to learn the subtleties of the precious Law, the timeless lessons of David and Solomon. It was only after he had begun to speak that he stole a final glance at Saul moving sprightly to his appointed task, his long red hair bouncing too fervently upon his shoulders.

ate in the morning of the fourth day, after the crucifixion of Jesus of Nazareth, Thomas came home. He arrived with Mark, who had found him praying unobtrusively in a forgotten corner of the Temple, kneeling, with the shock of the Master's death spilled upon his face. The other ten disciples jumped up to greet the Twin, as he was sometimes called, and surrounded him while chattering all at once. The women fussed over him and sat him down for some food and drink. The hard-faced disciple was beloved by his brethren and the Galilean women, in spite of his gloomy nature, as they were often humored by his overly pessimistic demeanor. They knew that Thomas overflowed with a prickly, perpetual angst, and would always anticipate the worst in everything. Still, underneath his anxious exterior, a heart of extraordinary courage beat in near concert with the Masters'.

At no time had that been more evident than when Jesus and the disciples had received a message from Lazarus' family in the recent spring that Lazarus was ill and close to death. The Twelve were concerned that if Jesus returned to Bethany, just two miles from Jerusalem, he would be seized by his enemies and stoned to death. In fact, they might all be seized and stoned. After receiving that message, Jesus stayed for two more days in the place where they were encamped. This had pleased the Twelve; for they had believed that the Nazarene would hurry to Bethany if he was indeed going to heal his sick friend. Then, on the third morning, in that place in the wilderness, Jesus had startled them by saying, "Let us go to Judea again." Naturally, the Twelve were not in accordance. Why would he seek to return to Bethany to see a deathly ill man in plain sight of the Temple where his bitterest enemies held court? And then Jesus had told them, "Lazarus is dead. And I am glad for your sakes that I was not there, that you may believe. Nevertheless, let us go to him."

Now, the Twelve knew that the Master could not be persuaded to stay away from Jerusalem. When the Nazarene spoke out his decisions, no one was ever capable of influencing his appointed plans. But they were also absolutely sure that, if Jesus returned to Bethany, he would be captured and killed. And so they congressed together away from him and cowered in fear before Thomas stood up before them to exclaim, "Let us also go, so that we may die with him." It was at that precise moment that the Twelve had come to see just how deeply his true love for Jesus reclined in the courageous heart of their melancholic brother.

They sat around him in a circle and Peter spoke first. "Thomas, the Lord Jesus has risen, just as He said He would do. He is alive and back among us! He appeared to the Magdalene yesterday morning, and then to me in the afternoon in an olive grove on the road to Bethany. After that, to Cleopas and his friend on the way to Emmaus, and then, to all of us last evening, right here, in this very room. He is as alive as when we last were with Him— His wounds still evident, but alive. He ate a little of the fish that is on your plate," said the exuberant leader as he pointed to the meal that had been prepared for Thomas. The other disciples were just as exhilarated. They were eager to share the news of the resurrection with Thomas but he was hard pressed to pick out a whole recounting in the nonsensical babble that filled the Upper Room. And Thomas would not, could not, join in with their enthusiasm. He was brokenhearted and shattered by the one fact that he knew was true—that Jesus of Nazareth had been nailed to a cross by the Romans in Golgotha on Thursday, where he had hung till his death on that afternoon. He was devastated by the Master's death, and did not even wish to be here with his friends as they attempted to make him feel better with their far-fetched tales.

"Leave me alone in my grief so I may heal my ravaged gut. Please leave me alone. I wish I had died with him or was, at least, still at the Temple in prayer for his soul. Please—stop telling me these lies!" So he said unto them, "Unless I see in his hands the print of the nails, and put my finger into the print of the nails, and my hand into his side, I will not believe!"

The disciple John was not going to give in to Thomas' stubborn disbelief without engaging him directly. "Thomas," he cried out, "look at my eyes. I tell you, the Lord Jesus, the Christ, rose from His tomb and came to us all last night. He spoke to us. We touched Him. We saw His wounds, the healing jagged wounds filled with His blood. You must believe me!"

And, even though the other ten disciples, and Cleopas, and Mary of Magdala continued to tell him the stories of their encounters with the Risen Christ, Thomas did not believe. He would simply not be convinced unless he saw Jesus with his own eyes and touched the Lord with his own hands. Finally, Peter raised his right hand as a signal to stop the repeated attempts to convince Thomas of the resurrection of their Rabbi Jesus. It was futile to continue; in fact, it would probably harden Thomas' disbelief, which stood as thick as the stone laid Temple walls. This was Thomas. "That is enough, my friends," said the firm leader, "let us be happy that Thomas is back home with us, safe and healthy. We shall remain here in prayer and worship and await another visit from the Risen Christ." He walked over to where Thomas was forlornly sitting and lifted the smaller man up off his seat and into his arms and said, "Welcome home, my friend."

Thomas let go of his emotions in the stronger man's grasp. He could feel the coarse strands of Peter's robe as they cut through the tears that ran down his trembling cheeks. The others rose quickly to touch the two men upon their shoulders. For the longest time, the only sounds that broke the silence were the muffled, captive croaks escaping from Thomas's swollen throat. And, even though he did not believe a word of their fantastical stories, it felt good to release his grief into that shared embrace. It felt good to be back among his brothers. It felt so good to be home.

It was the custom of the Jewish pilgrims to stay in Jerusalem for the seven days of unleavened bread, and prayers that followed the Passover. Saul of Tarsus had spent the whole week among the pilgrims, carefully listening to the rumors and innuendos that swept through the Temple grounds and into the streets of the capital. On Friday, or eight days to the hour since the final words of the Rabbi from Nazareth were uttered from his cross, Saul strode to Annas' home to speak with the High Priest, Caiaphas, and his father-in-law.

The two powerful priests were in repose in Annas' courtyard, enjoying a well earned respite from their ceremonial duties at the Temple during that Holy Week. Neither of them rose when Saul was announced, but Caiaphas motioned for his servant to pour the young Pharisee a healthy dose of sweet wine, and offered him some honey encrusted dates that swam in their own sticky juices. In just three hours, the sun would set on the city and the Holy Week, and a new Sabbath would commence. The High Priest would bid the pilgrims farewell in services tonight at the Temple, but then invite them to return to the Temple in forty two days for the Feast of the Pentecost—a celebration of the first wheat harvest in the Promised Land after the Hebrews had escaped the chains of their Egyptian captors. Although he had a detailed report to give to the High Priests, Saul settled back into his chair rather than to risk upsetting the contented air that leisurely drifted through the stunning blooms and green stems of Annas' prideful garden. The wine was exquisite, but could only hope to accompany the sumptuous taste of the sweetened dates like a plump bridesmaid combing the long hair of a beautiful bride. Naturally, it was Caiaphas who spoke first. "Tell us, my friend, what are the people saying in the streets of our great city."

The zealous scribe set his ornate goblet down carefully on a handcrafted side table. "My lords," he began, while bowing his forehead slightly forward to give respect, "there are a hundred rumors and tales in the streets of our fine city. Some of them believe the truth—that the body of the Nazarene was stolen by the Galileans to fulfill their Master's prophecies. Yet others claim that this Jesus, the Messiah, no less, rose from his tomb and has been seen in the city, preaching and teaching as if his crucifixion was but a dream." Saul smiled at the priests and shook his head ruefully. "Everyone is arguing—but even the believers have a difficult task in explaining how their mighty Messiah found himself hanging from a cross, if he is so all powerful. Yet we must be vigilant, for Jerusalem remains a tinderbox waiting for a spark to ignite an uncontrollable fire."

"Where are the Galileans? Where are those who traveled with him, and what are they saying?" queried a suddenly serious Annas.

"The disciples of the Rabbi are in a merchant's home in the Upper City," answered Saul, "and I have not seen one of them in the streets since the first day of the week. With all due respect, and since they are not breaking the Law in any way, I have not had them brought before you for preaching the blasphemous teachings of their Master."

Caiaphas nodded his agreement. "Yes, we cannot afford to have them arrested unless they break the Law. We could have an uprising in the streets, which the Romans would quell with swift violence. But, Saul, they cannot remain in the home forever; the day may soon be upon us when they must come out to confirm the rumors in the streets. And you will be there with the full power and authority of the Sanhedrin and Governor Pilate at your call!"

"Indeed, I have spoken with the Governor in confidence," affirmed Annas, "and he continues to support our efforts to avoid any insurrections among the common people that could come to the attention of Rome and Emperor Tiberius. We may request his aid, if needed, just as we did last week, when we brought the Rabbi to trial for blasphemy against our God."

"My lords, my passion for destroying these Galileans in their blasphemy equals my love for the Torah and the purity of our Laws," said the red headed Saul with eyes blazing with an immoderate intensity. "I shall not rest until I extinguish this threat to our most cherished beliefs, our customs, and to our sacred Temple. This, I promise you." And, while speaking this, he laid his hand upon his heart.

Caiaphas was reminded again of the wisdom in their selection of that young man. This is one that Gameliel taught beautifully—a true son of Israel. The High Priest chose a sweetened date and swirled it about in the warm honey. He savored the flavor with his eyes closed and then allowed the wine to cleanse his palate. "Well, it has been eight days since this Jesus was crucified, and five days since his body was stolen. Perhaps, we have averted a situation—perhaps the worst is behind us," said a hopeful Caiaphas.

Saul rose to take his leave. He intended to visit the Temple before the sun set on the Holy Days, to gauge, once more, the mood of the pilgrims. "In the name of Abraham, and the twelve tribes of Israel, I hope that your spoken words become the truth," he replied to Caiaphas. The Pharisee bowed to the High Priest and turned his attention to Annas, who was tending to an unruly plant whose beauty was speckled with brown leaves that were dying between its thorns. He left without speaking to the powerful patriarch, but not before noticing that Annas was less hopeful than his son-in-law. Only the blood of an aged thumb, nicked open by a wayward thorn, distracted the old man from mumbling his dissent and speaking out in disagreement.

It was a short walk from Annas' home to the main entrance of the Temple. The pilgrims, who had been living in Jerusalem for over a week, were preparing to journey back to their homes on the first day of the new week. Families everywhere were preparing for the Sabbath, and gathering their belongings— many of them would leave Jerusalem at sunset on Saturday and travel in the cool, night air by the swinging illumination of hand held lanterns. The others would leave in the morning light of Sunday. Saul marveled at the pilgrims from so many different nations, and the way they prepared to leave the city. "I must heed the ones who stay behind, for they will be the rebels," he thought. Saul walked through the middle of the bustling pilgrims with the confidence of a much larger man. The knowledge that he was working in alliance with the Almighty God for the people of Israel, put a bounce in his bowlegged gait.

"My father would be proud to see me in this appointment. Yes, I was well groomed by Rabbi Gamaliel, and my stern father, to be the one to save Israel from this attack on her birthright. Thanks be to God that I have been called to lead this battle against these transgressors; for I shall never waver from doing all that I can to keep my people pure in the Law and beholden to the sacrifices of our ancestors."

To Saul's left, as he approached the Holy Temple, stood the stairway that rose into the Court of the Gentiles. Herod's builders had doubled the size of the enclosed area, and surrounded it with an elaborate Hellenistic portico. On the second to the top step of the stairs, stood a man passionately speaking in Greek to an animated group of men who surrounded him. Saul jostled his way to the front of the circle and slid sideways between two larger men, to have an unimpeded look at the speaker. At first view, the sheer beauty of the man stunned Saul. He was beardless, with closely cropped, light hair that encircled a glowing countenance seemingly carved from the smoothest marble in the capital. The speaker's eyes were hypnotically azure, and Saul listened to him speak for minutes before he could even comprehend the meanings of those spoken words. It was as if the mythical Greek God Apollo had left his home in Olympia to return to speak directly to these people. His voice was as smooth as the honey that he could still taste in his mouth. His presence was powerful, yet gentle, like the quiet roar of a river that flows without impediments. His white, silk robe seemed to beat in perfect rhythm, as the golden threads that bordered his robe fluttered in a coupled dance with his exhortations. But the words of that beautiful man startled Saul back from his poetic absorption.

The Greek was speaking about that Jesus, the "Christos," the Messiah—telling his people that a great man had been crucified. He listened intently as Stephen fluently linked the words and acts of the Nazarene to God's original call to Moses, and to the prophets of Israel, that had been disparaged in their own time. "How was it possible that this Jesus charlatan could fool this educated man, just as he did with the rabble of Galilee? Surely, I understand how the clever Rabbi exploited his signs and healings to sway the simpleminded," thought Saul, "but this is the first formally educated man that I have seen who believes in this tripe—this twisted gibberish!"

A hidden wave of portended fear swept through Saul's being like the shadow of a skittering rat. He shuddered with distaste. "Perhaps I am in a tougher battle than I assumed" he thought. "I can arrest any man, but I cannot jail their convictions nor shackle their ideas behind impenetrable walls." And so, Saul challenged him. "My good man, you speak so eloquently, but I must question the wisdom of your words. Why do you speak so reverently of one who was lawfully tried and crucified by our Elders of the Sanhedrin?"

The handsome Stephen looked down upon his questioner. He smiled as he answered, "I speak only of that which is righteous and virtuous in the eyes of the Lord."

"But surely you cannot yoke the one who led our people from slavery in Egypt to a common criminal who defiled the very land upon which he hung above, nailed to a cross. Why did God not protect him as he protected Moses from his enemies if this Jesus, as you say—is the Christos?" said a more visibly frustrated and angered Saul.

And yet, Stephen did not respond in kind with sharpened or raised voice. Instead, he surveyed the group of riveted men who formed a crescent at his feet, and then spoke intimately, "The answer that you seek lies in the words of our prophets. The ways of our enemies never change—do we not still wear the chains of our days in slavery around our hearts when we fail to recognize the One who was here among us?"

Saul fixed his baleful eyes upon the angelic face of the undaunted Greek. With authority, he hissed, "And you should be very careful that you do not join him in an early death, my friend. Your handsomeness and your melodious voice will not save you if you continue to speak against our Law."

Again, Stephen just smiled and continued on with his discourse with the men. A discourse that drew his audience closer with every word. An infuriated Saul turned upon his heels and, unhesitatingly, exited the throng in the direction of the Hebrew Temple. He did not glance back to see if his veiled threat had broken the spell that the Greek so obviously held over his small audience. "No, there is no need to look backwards—I will see this one again if he continues to chirp and strut, like a peacock, to the people. I do hope he understands that the only songs ever sung in Golgotha are wrenching lamentations."

ight days, and seven full evenings, had passed since the Galileans had last seen the Risen Christ. As Peter had requested, their days had been filled with prayers and worship to God, the Father, in the name of Jesus. It was natural that they remained in fear for their lives, and still unsure as to the reality of exactly what they had witnessed. They wondered privately, despite having seen Jesus eating the prepared fish of eight evenings hence with their own eyes, if they had only viewed an apparition, a ghost, instead of the Risen Christ. Nonetheless, the cornerstone of the Church, the Lord Jesus Christ, was now being remembered in the private meals they shared by candlelight in the Upper Room of their protected home. John and the Magdalene had fashioned the ceremony from the instructions previously given to them by the Master. They would begin with a blessing on the food and a simple hymn or two. Then, Peter would lead them in focused prayers, asking for the Lord's coverage over them, by remembering what Jesus had told them during their last meal together—"Most assuredly, I say to you, whatever you ask the Father in My name, He will give to you." And so they prayed together in community and were forthright in placing their entreaties at the foot of the Cross, so that their prayers could be hand delivered to the Almighty God in the resurrection of His Chosen Son. And to conclude, they would recite the model prayer that the Lord had taught them, and then eat the blessed food in remembrance of His life—the bread representing His body and the wine, the blood of the new covenant with the Kingdom of God. There was a shared wholeness in worshiping together in song, prayer and meal, with one voice rising from their dinner table to the Lord. This was the voice of a reborn Israel, free in spirit at last.

On the eighth evening since their last visit from the Risen Christ, a spirited squabble arose among the Galileans, as to what they should be called in the streets of Jerusalem. "Let them call us the Princes in the Royal Court of the New King of Israel," said the headstrong young John, "so that we may be known as the ones who shall now wield the power in Jerusalem."

"But you are not even a Prince in this home," Thomas cried out, while allowing a rare smile to momentarily brighten his somber mood. "No, we should be known as the Nazarenes—disciples of the One who was born in the City of David, and who sought and found His disciples in Galilee."

"You are both wrong!" thundered a mirthful Peter, "for there will be others who will join with us with their baptism in the living water. Our home, this Church—will be open to all Jews who believe in the message and the death and resurrection of the Risen Christ." Peter opened his arms wide to signify his welcome to those who would enjoin with them in spirit and deed. "We cannot have a nation of princes, nor bring others to the Lord by forcing them to be called after that poor, mud ridden outpost we know as Nazareth. Can we? I tell you—you are both wrong!" As usual, the men quickly picked sides and their voices rose in matching volumes, as they vehemently argued for their chosen position.

Neither a compromise was forged, nor a new name proposed until a single, female voice cut through the bedlam with the clarity of a hawk's cry, crisply slicing through the air of a cold winter's night. "We are the Followers of the Way," said the Magdalene with the confidence of a woman who had touched the Messiah.

"What do you mean, Mary?" said Peter as the fever of the tumult broke into a hushed silence. "Pray, please tell us."

Mary gathered her robe about herself and spoke in a tone that did not seek argument. "He came to show us the Way to find the Kingdom of God. He died on that Cross in Golgotha to show us the Way to respond to those who will always deny God's Kingdom as they seek the treasures of this world above all else. And He rose beyond death from that dark tomb to show us the Way to everlasting life."

The men and the other women sat in a stunned silence. No one said a single word until Peter spoke at last. "So it shall be. We are the Followers of the Way, and we shall build a Church in the name of our Lord Jesus Christ." Everyone spoke their approval, and John rose to give a blessing to the food that was being placed before them. Tonight, they would pray with the powerful energy of those who understand their mission. So, John blessed the food to their nourishment and asked that the offered food and wine give them the strength to follow their revealed way, and to build the Church that must be built. He prayed that they would find the courage to do that in the face of their enemies, who, he knew, stood unopposed in the Temple and in control of the streets outside the door of their borrowed home—the contented and corrupted Sanhedrin and those who represented the full glory and power of the Roman Empire.

Then, just as John finished with a gentle hand wave above the food, Jesus was there amongst them again. Standing erect and smiling without any evidence of having climbed up the stairs or arriving in a way that they could understand. He was just there, alive, as the Risen Christ and vibrating His love in their midst. "Peace to you," He said, while looking over all of them like the vigilant shepherd watching over the sheep that He had often portrayed in parables. This time, the Eleven were not fearful and were so happy to see Him. Then He walked over to a startled Thomas, stood before him, and looking into his eyes, said, "Reach your finger here, and look at My hands; and reach your hand here, and put it into My side. Do not be unbelieving, but believing."

And then a trembling Thomas could see the fresh wounds of Jesus just inches from his touch. Despite knowing, in his heart, that the man who stood in front of him was indeed the Risen Christ, he did as he was told, and had wished, and placing his hands inside the wounds, his fingers could feel the Master's heartbeat in the flesh of the still healing wounds. Then Thomas, collapsing to his knees in humility, exclaimed to Him, "My Lord and my God!"

Jesus, looking down upon his faithful servant, who now knelt in full surrender to the truth that stood above him, smiled. He then placed one hand upon Thomas's quivering cheek and said, in a voice that filled the Upper Room, "Thomas, because you have seen Me, you have believed. Blessed are those who have not seen and yet have believed."

The manservant announced to his Master, Joseph of Arimathea, who was sitting at his plush desk in the library of his Jerusalem lodgings, "Sir, the High Priest, Caiaphas, and another man are here to see you."

"Very well, please see them into this study." Joseph put down his writing pen and swept away the commercial papers that detailed the intricate dealings of his vast business holdings in the tin and metals trade. As instructed by the High Priest, during his last appearance before his colleagues of the Sanhedrin, he had sent his family home to Arimathea and had intended to defend his actions, once again, at their scheduled meeting on that Sunday, the first day of the week. "What does the High Priest have to say to me that requires a visit to my home?" he thought.

His curiosity was interrupted by the grand arrival of the High Priest, alongside Saul of Tarsus. Caiaphas marched into the study as if he was the rightful owner of the splendid room. "Joseph," Caiaphas began, "You remember meeting my young friend, Saul, at the Temple a fortnight ago, don't you?"

"Yes, of course," said the respected merchant, while rising to greet his guests and motioning to his servant to prepare some refreshments. "And to what do I owe the pleasure of this visit?"

"A simple question that seeks an honest answer," replied Caiaphas, as he took the offered seat and arranged his priestly robe to splay over the edges of the luxuriant chair. He stroked his right index finger on the sharply stitched line where the precious wood met the silken fabric. "My good man, we have thought long and hard about your curious decision to bury the body of the Nazarene, a few weeks ago, in your own private tomb. Nonetheless, we must take you at your word, since you are a respected member of the Sanhedrin, and a prominent businessman in much of the Roman Empire. Still, we must ask you something that has remained in our thoughts like a thorn buried deep in one's thumb. I thought it best to ask you man to man, in the company of a witness." Caiaphas finished by waving his hand in the direction of the sitting scribe, who remained mute in his seat.

"Go on," replied Joseph.

"Let me be blunt. Were you a follower of this Jesus? Did you have a relationship with him before his death at the hands of the Romans?" blurted out an agitated Caiaphas.

"Caiaphas, and to you too, Saul, let me be clear, so that you will understand my position on this matter in full clarity. First of all, let me remind you that I was not in agreement with the Council's original decision to seek the Nazarene's execution by Governor Pilate's decree. I am a businessman, and a devout Jew, who worships our Almighty God and the tenets of our Law as so beautifully inscribed in our Torah, and I saw no need to vote with the majority on this matter," said Joseph, while pouring them each a goblet of his finest wine. "I thought I had explained this to you during my appearance in front of the Sanhedrin—I knew of the Rabbi, and I had heard him speak and answer questions in the Temple, and simply believed that he deserved the proper burial due any member of the Twelve Tribes. I am sure even the esteemed Rabbi Gamaliel would agree with my understanding of our customs in this matter." At the mention of his teacher, Saul returned Joseph's gaze, but did not offer his opinion.

A small, brightly colored bird landed on the sill of an open window, and the three men watched it flutter and scratch its claws on the darkened wood in the uncomfortable silence. The conversation did not continue until the bird flew away.

"Well, my learned friend, I cannot say if I believe that you are speaking the whole truth," said a wary, cautious Caiaphas, "but I thank you for receiving us and offering us this fine wine. Now, I do hope that you are telling us the truth; for even a man as respected as you for his goodness will not survive the vengeance of his colleagues at the Sanhedrin, if they were to find out otherwise." The High Priest took a finishing swig of his refreshment and then fixed his eyes upon Joseph. "You do understand, Joseph. The body of the charlatan was stolen by his friends from Galilee. If we find the body, or discover that you have aided them in any way, then you will suffer the consequences that they will suffer. Death, my old friend, is too good for them, as it is for anyone who challenges the God of Israel with such utter blasphemies! These fools will make a mistake soon in our city, and we will strike with the swiftness and ruthlessness of King David's armies."

"Of course, Caiaphas, I understand. But I am merely a simple man, content in following our Law and offering my aid and mercy to those in need," said Joseph, while standing to bid them farewell. "I thank you for your kind words of caution." Joseph watched his guests as they left his lodgings and began their walk back to the Temple. The taller, regal Caiaphas was in the lead, clearly energized by the youthful presence of Saul of Tarsus. The younger man had not spoken at all during the entire visit but a zealous authority now introduced itself in his purposeful walk. As Joseph watched their conversation from afar, it seemed as though Saul was questioning an underling, instead of accompanying the High Priest of Jerusalem as a witness. Joseph watched the two of them until they shrank from his sight. "True believers, those two, but probably not a real threat to me. Unless, of course, they find a way to look inside my very heart."

n the two weeks that followed the Risen Christ's second appearance to the Eleven and the others in the locked safety of the Upper Room, the disciples began to feel the confidence to move about the city without the threat of capture, by either the ever watchful spies of the Sanhedrin or the soldiers of Imperial Rome. There were others in the streets that were starting to believe as they did, and they shared with these known friends from Galilee the stories of having seen Jesus alive again. Quietly, privately, they shared the good news with tempered passion. And they greeted their like hearted friends with a kiss of peace, as all available monies were pooled and shared to buy the food necessary to keep the followers of the Way in Jerusalem, as they awaited the coming Pentecost. The peace kiss sealed their collective commitment to their Lord Jesus, and their new way of living. It served as an unspoken rebuttal to the kiss that Judas Iscariot had placed, in betrayal, upon the Master's cheek. Now everyone was welcome to share the evening meal at dusk in the Upper Room with the Eleven, and the women and guests from Galilee. Furthermore, everyone was encouraged to participate in the worship ceremony which convened around the central table. The shared meal was a pure expression of brotherly love, and the richer visitors delighted in bringing food and wine for all of the attendees to enjoy. They memorialized Jesus in the very way that He had shown in His last supper with the disciples before His arrest and crucifixion. The disciples often spoke in worship, after the food had been blessed and the songs sung, by retelling the ancient stories of their people and recalling the spoken words and challenging parables of their Rabbi.

One evening in the Upper Room, John was speaking to those that were gathered. The young man's countenance gleamed in remembrance of an answered query by his now Risen Lord, the Christ. "And when He had silenced the Sadducees," spoke John to all in attendance, "a Pharisee, a lawyer, asked Him this question to test Him, 'Teacher, which is the great commandment in the Law?' Now, according to the Pharisees, there are 613 commands in the Law, and we all know that they follow every one of them to perfection," revealed John, while allowing a gentle laugh to encircle the table. "They were trying to trick Him, but Jesus answered him as a teacher revealing a solution to a student. So He said to the Pharisee that 'You shall love the Lord your God with all of your heart, with all of your soul, and with your entire mind. This is the first and great commandment. And the second is like it. You shall love your neighbor as yourself. On these two commandments hang all the Law and the Prophets.'"

A young brother from Galilee spoke from his place on the wall to ask, "I ask of you, John, did this satisfy the lawyer?"

John replied, "The Pharisees will observe a gnat without

seeing the camel upon which it sits. The Rabbi pointed out to them that God willed the Law to hang upon these two commandments of love, and so, too, for the 613 commands, or the Ten given to Moses in the Exodus—each which must bloom from this root." John looked to the young devotee who had asked the question, and when their eyes met above the circle of the seated disciples, he concluded, "The lawyer and his friends were astonished, speechless; but they could not disagree or battle with words against His wisdom. There are men here at this very table who can witness to the truth of my memory."

When the benediction was prayed and the worship ceremony was over, the Magdalene sought out John to speak to him in the privacy of a small courtyard that was illuminated by a near full moon, shining brightly on that late April evening. The clay bricked, open garden descended from the rear of the home of Mark's father, and they sat together upon a sturdy bench under the one palm that broke the falling moonlight into unequal shafts. Mary regarded the young disciple with a woman's eye. "I see that he is maturing and losing his natural arrogance and pride. And in that void I see a tolerance budding—an understanding of the mysteries of loving freely without intention—expecting nothing in return but the hope of reflected love. Yes, John is softening, like one of these clay bricks dipped in a river, losing his hard edges until he will be carried downstream by the current of the Master's love."

"John, I was approached at the market this morning by the manservant of Joseph of Arimathea," said the Magdalene, "with a message from our friend Joseph."

"And, pray tell, what did Joseph want of you?" John replied, with a bit of surprise in his voice.

Mary continued, "The manservant spoke in confidence to me and delivered a private message from Joseph. Joseph believes that we must leave Jerusalem at once. There are forces in the Sanhedrin that are planning our immediate arrest. Joseph's servant apologized that his master could not deliver this message in person, saying that Joseph felt it was far too dangerous for us to be seen in each other's company."

"Well, Mary, do you believe this to be truly the words of Joseph of Arimathea? Have you relayed this message to Peter?" said John.

"Yes, I spoke to Peter at once," she replied.

John was pleased that Mary had gone directly to their leader. Peter would weigh the words with great attention and decide what was in the best interest of the Eleven, and the rest of the Galileans. "And what did Peter say to you, Mary?"

"We are to push off in the light of the early morning. Peter says that we shall journey to Nazareth, to take Mother Mary to James and the rest of Jesus' brothers. He is upstairs now, telling everyone the time for our leaving."

"And what of Jesus, will He know that we are in Galilee?" cried out John, in fear of missing another visit from the Risen Christ.

Mary smiled at her friend and reached out to touch his arm and said, "The Lord knows where we are at all times, John. Come; let's get ready to go home."

On the Sabbath of the week in which Peter led the Galileans out of Jerusalem and home to the safe sands of Galilee, the young Hellenist, Stephen, sat by himself on the steps of the Synagogue of the Freedman. This Synagogue served as a meeting place for those of Jewish descent born outside of Israel. The Hellenists often worshiped in the Holy Temple, to attend sacrificial worship ceremonies or to celebrate the Jewish feasts. On this day though, Jews from Cyrenia, Alexandria, Cecilia, and all of Asia would congregate here at that Synagogue to confess their faith in the One God, pray, read Scripture from the Law and the prophets, and listen to a sermon preached in Greek, their mother tongue. Stephen was to present a reading on this Sabbath from the life of Moses; it was the account when the Lord appeared to him in the form of a burning bush, declared Himself to be the God of his fathers, of Abraham, Isaac, and Jacob, and implored the trembling, eighty-year-old man to remove his sandals and stand, for he was now on holy ground. Stephen thought to himself, "I want my brethren to remember that the Lord God is free to reveal Himself whenever, and wherever He might choose. And when He does, the ground beneath the revelation will be forever holy, for those who stand upon it in obedience. This is the way of the Lord." The young, handsome Hellenist held firm in his hands, a scrolled Septuagint, the Greek translation of the Hebrew Old Testament. He looked down upon the precious scroll and pressed the worn parchment against his heart. He knew well the stories of the Kings and of those who spoke the divine prophecies into the Torah. He understood how the Law was born, during the long exodus of the twelve tribes of Israel, and then came of age upon their arrival in the Promised Land. And Stephen was humbled that he had also been blessed by the Lord with beauty, a sharp mind, and the ability to express himself with a bold passion that released an unchecked charisma. He was ordained with a rare brilliance to be a powerful witness for the Almighty—one who believed and sang his faith from the very core of his soul. And yet, sitting on these old stones, Stephen knew that his truest power came not from these formidable, and God given gifts, but from the Word itself. The timeless power of the written Word passed down from generation to generation in spoken recitations that chronicled their people's history in stories that shared and exalted the same father and mother. The father; the inextinguishable love from God to His people, and the mother; the struggles to find the impenetrable path of love, of service, of obedience, and of surrender. "And now," he thought,

"I sit here with this scroll containing so many truths, beating as if alive next to my heart, knowing that the prophecies have come full circle. A King was born, was crucified and was sacrificed like the spring lamb on the altar in the Temple. But this lamb, this Jesus of Nazareth, would not simply bleed blood into a priest's chalice so designed to be pleasing to the Lord for He is of the Lord. He is His Son. He shed His own blood. The Son of Man who had come to show us the way to the Kingdom of Heaven which lies in every person's heart—in my own heart. Jesus is the Messiah! The sacrifice of His life—His surrender unto death; to reconcile us with our God, beyond the grasping claws of our constant sin, if only we repent. If only we seek the redemption that arises together with the dawn of every morning, just as the Baptist said in the first scorching heat of the desert between bites of dead locusts—'Repent, for the Kingdom of Heaven is at hand!' He has come." Stephen took the Septuagint away from his heart and held it in his hands, which rested across his seated thighs. Something was happening to him. He knew it. One cannot know and remain the same. A new energy was coursing through his veins, and his understanding tripled inside of him. He ran one hand through the closely cropped curls of his uncovered head and stood up gingerly to enter the Synagogue as the time had come for the worship service to begin. As he covered his head, men from cities across the known world were making their way down the streets and into the Synagogue.

The dialects of the foreign cities melted away into the streets as the men greeted each other in their common Greek language. "Now, what am I to say today in this Synagogue," he wondered, "since I know that the ancient prophesies have come true—am I to enter these doors and speak only words that will be pleasing to the elders? Am I to pretend that what has happened here in Jerusalem is of no consequence to our lives? Am I to pretend that I am unaware that the Messiah has come at the appointed time?" A single voice brought the answer.

"Stephen? My friends tell me that is your name," called out the diminutive man with long red curls, who had accosted him, during his preaching to a select group of Hellenistic friends, more than a fortnight ago. Stephen could see that he was no more than thirty years old, perhaps only a year or two beyond his own age. "Do you remember me? I spoke to you a few days ago when you were preaching on the steps at the Temple. Please, let me properly introduce myself, I am Saul, of Tarsus."

"Good day, my lord," said Stephen while recognizing the formal education reavealed in the clipped dialect of Saul's spoken Greek. "Are you coming to observe the Sabbath with us today? Please, come as my guest."

"No, I am on my way to the Temple to observe the Sabbath. I thank you for your offer, but I have responsibilities to fulfill for the High Priest, Caiaphas," said the proud Pharisee. "I am glad to see you, though, as I have a question to ask of you."

Stephen replied, "Of course, how may I be of service?"

Saul fixed a baleful stare upon the seductive eyes and striking features of the young Hellenist. "My friends also tell me that that you continue to publicly speak of this Jesus as if he were a great Rabbi, and not the cunning criminal who blasphemed our God and challenged the very pillars of our Law. So, I ask you my friend, did you not hear my warning to you at our previous meeting? Do you not know of the authority that allows me to speak so forthrightly to you?"

Stephen regarded Saul as the poisonous anger spilled out of the mouth of the smaller man. "Ah, he is versed in the Law, but caught in his own strict web of seeing only the obedience, while remaining blind to the love. Rigid. Unforgiving. Frightful." He thought as he carefully crafted his reply, "Yes, Saul. I heard your warning, but I speak only of righteous ways and the blessed fulfillment of the ancient prophecies. In the end, the people will decide the truth of these matters, won't they?"

The Pharisee dismissed that notion with an imperial wave of

his hand. "Stephen, they already decided and chose him over two other criminals for crucifixion. Now I will tell you once more. Be careful of what you speak. You do not want to end up like the Galileans, trapped in a home in the Upper City, and one foolish step away from following their so called Master unto his same death. After all, they cannot stay in their safe haven forever."

"But, my friend," replied Stephen, "the Galileans departed for their homes early on the second day of this week. They have returned to Galilee."

There was a long period of silence that came between them. Finally, Saul chose not to reply and turned upon his heels without a word of farewell. Stephen, too, turned away to walk up to the beckoning doors of the Synagogue. And only when he began to speak of Moses to the worshiping men, did he allow himself to forget the look that had come upon Saul's face when he had told him of the Galilean's journey—a look of pure surprise, watered by a withering hatred.

A lone wooden fishing boast cut peacefully through the still waters near the gray pebble shores of the Sea of Tiberius. Seven fishermen peered over the sides, squinting in search of fish rising to the crooked lamplight that illuminated the black waters under a shadowed moon. Their cast nets sat coiled and dripping at their feet, but were as empty as their growling stomachs; for they had not seen, nor netted, one fish in over seven hours of fishing. And yet, they were excited and free in their pursuit—Peter, the captain, his brother, Andrew, with their former fishing partners, John and James, the sons of Zebedee, and alongside Nathaniel, Phillip, and even a momentarily contented Thomas. No fisherman is ever happy when the expedition yields not a single fish but these men were at home gliding upon the fishing grounds of their youth, and far,

far away from the fear and intrigues that had threatened them in Jerusalem. They were accustomed to the occasional failure of netting a suitable catch, so they reveled in their companionship as their teasing banter glanced off the half slackened sail and skipped across the tranquil sea. "Ah, it is good to be home and fishing these waters," said Peter definitively, "but I see that I must find a younger crew if I am to eat in the coming days. Have you men lost your touch during our travels?"

The men all laughed heartily and turned to face the captain of their small boat. In the refracted light of the lanterns, Peter's robust frame shook in mirth and he reached forward to cuff his brother, Andrew, upon the back of his head. The quietest of them answered him promptly. "How can we catch any fish if our captain is always talking?" said the dour Twin. "The fish at the bottom of this sea can hear you roaring from twenty lengths away."

"I am yelling with pangs of hunger, my friend, and in knowing that I should starve if I am to depend on this crew to catch my breakfast. I ate better in Jerusalem, scrounging up a bit of bread wherever I could," cried out Peter.

James twisted about from his position, peering hopefully into the water and teased the cheerful captain. "You needn't worry too much, Peter, about your next meal. A marching Roman legion could live for weeks off that ample belly." He ducked away quickly as Peter threw a clump of ripened seaweed in his direction; it slammed against, and then sank slowly down, the curved wood to the right of James. The friendly teasing and banter continued until the dawn arrived and the men sailed the boat toward the shore at Capernaum. There would be no fish for breakfast that morning but each was satisfied with the sure bounty of the trip. They had a great fellowship floating in the freedom of the open sea; together, laughing and fearless— home. They would return to their families when they docked and set the time to go fishing in the dark moon of the next evening. Surely, they would find the new hiding places of their quarry—if they did not get too discouraged with the failure of tonight.

The disciple John stood tall in the front, looking for a safe route to guide the boat through hidden rocks as they skimmed their way to the shore. The early light of the dawn warmed him and granted him a clear visibility to chart their forward path. The ripples on the surface gleamed silver. Suddenly, John's concentration was disturbed by the misty silhouette of a bearded man standing under a single shade tree on the shore. He shielded his eyes with his hands to sharpen his vision, but could not recognize the stranger as a friend. "Friends, do you see that man on the shore under that tree over there," said John, as he pointed to the gray robed man who stood fixed in his place. The up twirling smoke from a charcoal fire wafted through the lower limbs and over the sea in their direction, and they could faintly smell the delicious aroma of cooked fish and warming bread. The smell roused their hunger, which sparked their curiosity as they scrambled about the deck to take a better look.

Peter stepped up next to John's position and he too shielded his eyes while peering at the man. "Perhaps he is seeking a ferry ride across the way. We should gladly offer him passage if he can pay us with a breakfast of grilled fish!" said Peter, as his crew unanimously declared their agreement. They guided the boat straight toward the man by the smoke of the fire, until they were close enough to speak.

The man raised his arms in greeting and said unto them, "Children, have you any food?" A somber disappointment swept over the men as they realized that the man was asking if they would sell a portion of their catch. They had not fish to sell. A man looking to buy fish was unlikely to have enough on hand to satisfy their hollow stomachs. Together, in unison, they shouted "No!" And then the man responded, calling out to them in a strong voice, "Cast the net on the right side of

Prison Book Project
P.O. Box 1146
Sharpes, FL 32959

the boat, and you will find some." So Peter, against his better judgment, yet in deference to his hunger, ordered his men to cast out the nets immediately. They had nothing to lose in the throwing of one more cast. Within three heartbeats, the nets were full of rolling, silver fish. There was no way that they could catch a week's worth of fish in one cast. The men were unable to draw them in due to the sheer size and weight of the haul. They held the full net against the side of the boat as they struggled to land, crabbing sideways by riding the crest of a wave tumbling close to the shore.

"Be careful," Thomas decried, as his reason fought in opposition against the groups' rising excitement, "to not tear the net and lose them all."

"I can't believe it—help me, I can barely hold up the net," said James, just as Andrew jumped to his side to help him. They were both stripped to the waist, and their muscles snapped taut as they used every ounce of their strength to hold the catch in place.

Now, John did not look in the direction of the bursting net, plump with the heavy catch, but kept his eyes locked on the man on the shore. He strained to see his face in a clearer focus and spoke in a whisper to himself. "Is it Him? Could it really be Him, here on this lake in Galilee? So close to the place where He first called us to disciple, to follow Him?" And then, as the man smiled at them, he recognized Him and knew, so he turned to Peter and spoke so loudly that all the crew could hear his words over the sounds of the incoming waves and the thrashing of the silver fish, "It is the Lord!" When Peter heard John's words ringing in the open air, he quickly slipped on his outer robe and plunged into the sea. He was not an accomplished swimmer, but the first wave took him toward his resurrected Savior, and he kicked and flailed his arms until his knees rested upon the smooth gray pebbles in the frothy surf of the shoreline. He stood up, breathing heavily from his exertion, and shook the captured water from his thick beard. Placing his hands in supplication, as if in prayer, he bowed to the Risen Christ.

Jesus said, "Come, bring some of the fish which you have just caught." Peter turned around in the returning white surf to find his men. The other six disciples were still struggling to bring the boat to shore as the fish laden net unbalanced the boat and kept them from following along the path of their selected line. Andrew and James still held the net to the side of the boat, but they were beginning to visibly tire. The other four paddled furiously on the other side but the weight of the captured fish caused the craft to circle in a lazy pattern toward the shore. So Peter jumped into the sea and pulled the net from the hands of his brother and James and dragged it to land. It was a feat of great strength, but the other disciples had seen him do that type of thing before when his passion erupted. Peter knelt down to inspect the net and was surprised to see it untorn, despite the enormity of the catch. The rest of the men then stumbled onto the shore and tied the boat off on a withered stump. Then, Jesus said to them, "Come and eat breakfast." Not one of the disciples dared to ask if He was Jesus, their Lord. Instead, they busied themselves in dragging the net to the charcoal fire. As they were counting the huge catch, one hundred and fifty three in all, Jesus reached down to take some fish and bread off the burning coals and gave the cooked bounty to the hungry disciples. What had seemed at one time to be only one fish on the coals, with a browning piece of bread, was now enough to serve each of the men an ample portion. When He served them, the men could see that the wounds on His hands and feet were healing, no longer jagged and pink, but brownish in color, and scarring with a tissue tougher than the surrounding skin. And so they knew that it was Jesus.

This was the third time that the Risen Christ had shown Himself to His disciples since He had been raised from the dead. They were no longer overwhelmed or frightened to be before Him; and they sat down to eat the breakfast as they had so often sat together in the past. Encircled about a cooking fire and listening to the spoken words of wisdom from their Rabbi, while slowing picking that day's meal apart with their fingers. They chattered as satisfied men do and then argued over how many fish they would salt away and how many they would sell. And when they had finished, and each of them sat back on the packed sand with full bellies, Jesus said to Peter, "Simon, son of Jonah, do you love Me more than these?" And with His right hand, He waved it to signify the boat and Peter's livelihood on the sea.

The question startled the large disciple. It hurt him. Of course, he loved the One he knew as the Messiah with far more intensity than the love he had for his boat and his business. Still, he answered with affection, "Yes, Lord; You know that I love You."

The Risen Christ opened his eyes slowly upon Peter and simply said, "Feed my lambs." And then, as each of the other disciples pondered the question to Peter, Jesus spoke again. He looked, again, directly onto Peter and said, "Simon, son of Jonah, do you love Me?"

A flash of anger swept through Peter, but he held that emotion in his heart. And in meeting the eyes of the Lord in fullness, Peter replied, "You know that I love You."

Jesus nodded His head. As He stared at the dwindling embers of the cooking fire, He spoke out, "Tend My sheep." The rest of disciples shifted uncomfortably in their places. It was evident to them that Jesus was imparting a lesson to Peter, but they were unsure of the meaning of His questions, and in His requested demands. For a third time, Jesus questioned Peter, "Simon, son of Jonah, do you love Me?"

Peter was grieved. Tears sprung to the back of his eyes, but he pushed down the sadness and swallowed the lump that had taken residence in his throat. This took him a moment, but he answered without anger, "Lord, You know all things; You know that I love You."

And then the Christ spoke to him with the intensity of the Cross. "Feed My sheep. Most assuredly, I say to you, when you were younger, you girded yourself and walked where you wished; but when you are old, you will stretch out your hands, and another will gird you and carry you where you do not wish." The Christ was telling Peter the death that he would one day experience to glorify the Lord. And in Jesus so telling him, forgiving him, restoring him and validating his position of prominence in the Kingdom, in the company of the others. It will be Peter, so said the Lord, who will lead these men forward to spread the news of the gospel; the good news of the resurrection. So it will be Peter who will hold the keys to expanding the Kingdom. "Follow Me," said the Lord. Peter rose to follow Jesus as they walked down the pebbled shoreline. By now, the sun was in the morning sky and the sea sparkled with vivid blues and greens.

John, too, arose from his place where he had reclined on the breast of his beloved Christ, and followed them from ten paces behind. Peter, seeing that, and still in a bit of shock over knowing the circumstances of his death, asked, "But Lord, what about this man?"

And Jesus said unto him, "If I will that he remain until I come, what is that to you? You follow Me!"

Peter understood that the Lord was imploring him to follow His will and not concern himself about His will for the others. The chastened leader turned back to look at his younger friend and fellow disciple. He said, "He has risen above the others to become my right hand. Look at him! Look at the way he loves our Lord. He walks with the confidence of a man reborn. So my destiny will be different—I will die as He died, crucified with arms stretched and girded on hard wood. But the Lord said that John will live. Yes, he will be the one who will tell this story to the world."

ark's mother opened the heavy door to answer the known knock. "Mary, praise be to God, you are back," she exclaimed as she brought the Magdalene into a sisterly embrace and kissed her on an offered cheek. "Come and sit with me, I have so much to tell you. Where are the others? Are you alone?"

Mary stepped into the cool house. It was a nice feeling to be back in the safety of their home, and one staircase away from where the Lord had appeared to them in the Upper Room. "Strange," she thought, "but this is the closest thing I have to a real home, now. I am so happy to be home." Then she said to Mark's mother, "The men are a half day's walk behind me. I was impatient to see you, so they sent me ahead with friends from Galilee to ask if they may rest here during the Feast of the Weeks, the Pentecost. They will be here by sunset—may we stay with you?"

"Of course," the older woman replied, "Oh Mary, it is so good to see you. Come, let's go to the garden and I will bring us two goblets of my husband's finest wine. He will not even know it is gone!" The women shared a laugh over the truth of her prediction. "Tell me, my child; is Mother Mary safe, back in Galilee? Is she well?"

"Our mother is fine. We took her home to see Jesus' younger brothers and spent time in the home of James. Jesus appeared to him before our arrival, and he is now a committed follower of the Rabbi, the Risen Christ—so devout now and humbled as the brother of the Messiah, a follower of His Way. He was kneeling in prayer during the whole of our visit."

The two women adjusted their robes and sat down gingerly on comfortable chairs in the date palm shade that spilled onto the garden porch. Mark's mother handed a goblet filled to the brim with a deep plum colored wine to the Magdalene. They sat in close quarters, face to face, with their knees extending beyond the others, and leaned forward to speak conspiratorially in between the quiet sips of the delicious drink. And then, for a moment, nothing was said, as they allowed the ruddy grape to swirl about freely in their palates. There are such pleasures in this life, if one takes the time to notice. Such delicacies, such gifts to open slowly, to realize, to hold dear. "Tell me of the others, Mary—the men."

"Well, I have much to tell you about those scoundrels," said Mary, in a teasing tone. "First, there is the story of them fishing over a whole night in Galilee. John told me that they were having so much fun, teasing each other for not catching a single fish. Even Peter was as jovial as they had ever seen him, free and happy, back on the fishing grounds. They had fished all night and caught nary a one. Then, in the early morning light, Jesus—yes Jesus, called out to them from the shore to cast their nets to the other side of the boat. Well, they did not know it was Jesus—but they did once the nets began to fill with fish!"

"Tell me more," begged Mark's mother.

Mary arched her back into her chair and stared directly into the kind eyes of her friend. It was time to tell others what she knew. "My friend, the men are becoming strong Rabbi's before my very eyes," she began. "Jesus was so patient with them for three years. He taught them everything He knew about the Kingdom of God, in stories and parables that cut right through the walls of their ignorance and stubbornness. And now, they are seeing Him beyond His death, which has proven to them that He is God—the Son—the One that they sang about in the Psalms. The One the prophets promised. Still, they remain stubborn to the whole truth of the Word, and some scales still cover their eyes. So the Lord is still teaching the final lessons. He is still patient, still loving. They ate a breakfast of fish together on that shore in Galilee, and He continued to speak of the Way—the Way of our Lord." She paused to take a sip of the aromatic wine, but continued with just a moment's pause. "Now, He is preparing them to take this good news to the whole world, and I will tell you, dear Mother, that they are becoming more confident men in every new sunrise. And I have been honored to be with them as they are coming to this understanding. They are seeing that the Lord is, indeed, the cornerstone, the Rock. I tell you—a Rock that these men will preach upon with passion in their bellies until their own deaths. The Rock of their very foundation, which He taught them, was in their hearts all along. This is what they will know when the scales in their eyes fall, finally, to the dirt and their ears open fully to the Word." The Magdalene allowed a prideful emotion to add power to her words, like the way one speaks when telling a secret to a close friend. She leaned forward to whisper what she had observed on the journey back to Jerusalem. "They are coming to know, to believe in the Messiah; for they have seen Him beyond the evidence presented to their eyes. They are coming to understand their destinies that they will forge in His name; for they have heard Him with ears that are no longer covered with fearful hands. And they are coming to know the truth of the Kingdom of God; for He has loved them in every step of their journey together," cried out Mary in passionate spurts. She paused for a moment to capture her breath so that she could speak out the deepest truth. "They have met their Lord and have let Him enter their hearts."

Mark's mother smiled maternally to the eyes of the Magdalene. A mother need not respond in words when she recognizes when love is speaking. The dialect is unmistakable, and the words bring a meaning that does not require a spoken affirmation. The older woman nodded her understanding, and let Mary's words hang in the air between them like bees full of nectar, lazily spinning in sated circles, and landing only in the center of the blooms, where the clear drops of nectar are visible even to the naked eye. In time, Mark's mother spoke. "Mary, there are many more Galileans in the capital now. Some want to become followers of the Way. You see, the story of His resurrection is spreading slowly, but surely. Even some of the Hellenists are speaking of the Nazarene with great respect. So we have continued the love feasts here in your absence. Behind these doors, we greet each other with a peace kiss. A kiss that holds the peace that has come upon us in knowing that He lives."

This news thrilled the Magdalene. So, the good news was spreading in the streets, even while the disciples were away in Galilee. But a quick moving shadow passed over her joy, and it took her three breaths to recognize the fear. She thought, "Our enemies are here in the most holy rooms of the Temple. Powerful and unchecked by even the thinnest cords of restraint. Are we courageous enough now in the hands of the Risen Christ to survive their scheming hatred?" So Mary asked, "And what of our enemies? Will the Eleven be safe in the streets outside, or free to visit the Temple to worship?"

Mark's mother rose quickly from her chair. "Come, let's go inside. We will need to make a visit to the city market this afternoon if we are to feed those men fresh from the road." She put an index finger to her lips to signal a silence and motioned for the Magdalene to follow her with her free hand. When they entered the home, she closed the door that led in from the garden porch and motioned for Mary to follow her into a cool room that was dark to the outside light. As their eyes adjusted to the darkened room, she spoke quietly to Mary, "It unsettles me to speak in the garden about our enemies. My husband had a brief conversation with Joseph of Arimathea at the Temple last week. Such a man he is, such generosity and bearing. The two of them have done some business together here in Jerusalem."

"And what did they discuss," asked the Magdalene with respect.

"Joseph told my good husband to be very wary of the young Pharisee, Saul. He enjoys the confidence of the Sanhedrin, even to the private chambers of the High Priest, Caiaphas. Joseph claims that he speaks with the authority of the High Priest, and that he is as deadly as a hidden viper, yet patient in finding the perfect time to strike."

The Magdalene shook her head from side to side to indicate that she did not know of him.

Mark's mother could not help but take notice of the unblemished beauty of the younger woman. She could see that Mary's skin had come alive with the passion of having seen the Risen Christ. With love and concern she pondered her words, "She is shining in her reverence, but still too young, and naive, to understand the naked power of the forces aligned against the Eleven, and the followers of the Way. The Sanhedrin, if they wished, could place them all on trial and sentence them each to a brutal death. And with just the mildest nod from Rome, they would all be crushed into a fine dust and spread out over the steaming desert." And so she said to Mary, "Joseph says that this Saul is planning a trap for the men, so you must tell them to be vigilant in their dealings and cautious in their words."

Mary regarded her gracious host with her newly sharpened eyes. She thought, "I am afraid that the time for caution has passed, sweet mother. You still think in the old way, as if they are afraid of men and stones and swords. If our Lord can rise from His own dark tomb, then shall they also rise up in courage for loving Him; for believing in His words and in His way?" Then she said, "Dear Mother, I know that you give this advice with the wisdom of your years. And I thank you for your concern. Still, the Eleven are different now. They know the Risen Christ as His selected disciples. He chose them and then taught them the Way. They are growing in the Word, and becoming less fearful of the powerful men who will not believe—who may never believe! — men who wish only to protect their grip over our people. They might tell you themselves, if they were here; the sharp edge of a Roman sword is powerless to wound what Christ has offered to us with his spilled blood! Our life—forever."

Mark's mother gathered a basket to carry home the meats, fruits, dates, and cheeses that they would barter for today in the noisy, open market. It was obvious that further conversation would not strip the Magdalene of her youthful idealism and passion. Gripping the basket by its curved interlocking handle, she replied, "Come Mary, let us go to the market. Brave men must still eat well, yes?"

"Yes, Mother" said the Magdalene, with a wry smile, "even the bravest and most pious of men are still men, and sure to find the marrow in every bone."

On the morning of the fortieth day after the resurrection of Jesus Christ, a single cock crowed in the early morning stillness within a rock's throw of where the Eleven were soundly sleeping in the safety of the Upper Room. The raucous cry did not stir a single one of them, and was quickly swallowed in the low sounds and grunts that men make when sleeping in tight quarters. They were in their adopted home in Jerusalem, physically replenished by their time in Galilee, and happy in spirit after another appearance by Jesus on the shores of their ancestral fishing grounds. The Lord had come back to them again; and they had enjoyed eating the grilled fish He had provided after their long night without a fish found tangled in the strands of their thrown nets. The disciple, John, was dreaming peacefully, curled up between his brother, James, and a low snoring Andrew. In that dream, he was dressed in a long, white robe, fishing and netting nearly a hundred fish in every cast of his net. When he looked to his left, he saw Peter standing at the front of his own boat, laughing with pleasure over his own plentiful catch. And behind him were the others, each in their own colored boat and riding the waves in a multitude of directions. The fish laden boats did not seem to sink with the weight of their captured bounties, nor threaten each other with splintering crashes. The sun seemed fixed in the sky, yielding warmth and comfort; and the winds were constant and filled their sails with power.

John would have easily caught a thousand fish, had not he been gently awakened by a voice calling out his name. With a sleepy regret, John departed from his dream and was startled to see the unmistakable eyes of the Lord boring into his through the darkness in the sealed room. "John, awaken the others and let us journey together to Bethany," said Jesus. "Gather up the Eleven and join Me in the street in the front of this home." John immediately arose and went about the requested task. He went first to Peter and survived his grumbles to tell him of the Lord's wish. Slowly, the others began to rise on their haunches and began to wipe away the sleep that clung like sticky honey to their slow opening eyes. John shook his brother awake, and then watched as the others each awakened the one sleeping closest to him. In a whisper to them all, John said, "The Lord was here. He wants us to accompany Him on a journey to Bethany. He is waiting for us now, in the street in front of this home."

Not a single one of them doubted the truth of his words, and they wordlessly began to put on their robes and strap their feet into their leather sandals. Even Peter, who notoriously woke up like a speared lion if disturbed in his slumber, was obedient to John's request and dressed as soundlessly as a summer cloud. In short time, they formed a single line and descended down the stairs without awakening the others. Many of the sleeping bodies were Galileans who had come to worship with them and sleep there while awaiting the coming Pentecost that would arrive in ten days time. The house, which had once slept twenty, was now home to over one hundred; and every empty space was filled with a new follower of the Way, curled asleep and waiting for the morning's light. Only the Magdalene was awakened by their movements but she silently secured the front door behind the last of them, a muttering Thomas, without even extending a morning greeting as they passed into the street. And there He was, sandaled and dressed in the simple robe of so many shared journeys. "Come, let us go to Mount Olivet, to Bethany," He said, and turned at once to walk in that direction. The others fell into clumps of two or three behind Him and walked through the still City without fear—for they were in His presence. For once, John stood in the rear of the Eleven, and allowed the others to move up to crowd about Jesus and pepper Him with questions. After a dozen inquiries were met with silence, Jesus stopped to regard them with a father's patient love but that did not stop their desire to know of His plans. When they had successfully walked past the pool and through the Northeastern Gate, He turned to them and scolded them gently to focus on the steps of their journey. As He spoke, the first rays of the Eastern sun illuminated their destination in a beautiful light, and Mount Olivet sparkled in the distance. "All will be known when we arrive in Bethany."

Still, John wondered, "Why Bethany; and why today? Yes, it is a village that seems to hold great meaning for the Lord. This is where He would so often come to pray alone in the gardens and olive groves of Mount Olivet. I remember when a woman anointed Him with expensive oil there, and we all complained about such an extravagant waste of money. But He chastised us and thanked her for anointing His body in advance of His burial. There were so many signs of what was to come, but we were too ignorant to understand, to find the meaning of His spoken words or solve the hidden lessons in His parables. And Bethany was the village where His friend, Lazarus, lived, and died, and lived again—raised back to life four days after his death, when Jesus called him from his tomb. We witnessed it with our own eyes! Why did we not understand that if He could raise Lazarus by praying to His Father, then He could live beyond

His own crucifixion by praying to His own Father? How could we have been so blind and stupid as to who He is? What kept us from seeing the truth of our Lord and the fulfillment of all the prophets' descriptions of the coming Messiah—when Micah spoke of a redeemer to be born in Bethlehem, when Isaiah saw that He would be conceived of a virgin from Galilee and was not just a man but 'God with us,' and when the Psalmists sang that He would be pierced for our transgressions. Now I see that the whole of the Law, the ancient spoken and remembered history of our twelve tribes, was all to prepare us for the One."

Jesus, and the eleven men, walked in an incline on the dusty road that led to the town of Bethany. As they climbed Mount Olivet, the air became cooler and easier to breathe, and the dust was replaced by cooling dew. There was an uncomfortable silence as they passed the Garden of Gethsemane. John stole a glance at Peter and James to see if they still felt the guilt he harbored for sleeping instead of comforting Jesus in that time before His arrest, when He was in throes of His deepest despair. Jesus had said onto them there, "My soul is exceedingly sorrowful, even to death. Stay here with Me and watch." But the disciples had slept like children. Yes, it was just as He said to us in the moonlight of that terrible evening, "The spirit indeed is willing, but the flesh is weak." In perhaps the only time He truly needed us, they had slept. Peter and James did not return his guilty glance but kept their focus straight ahead on the last steps upward to the meadow summit of the spring blushed mountain. From that leveled perch, they could see in all directions, beyond the Garden of Gethsemane and clear to the very gates of the Holy Temple in Jerusalem. They watched the city awaken to just another day, but were far too high in the sky to hear the sounds of commerce, as the vendors called out their wares and the people scurried about in desperate fulfillment of their daily needs. Here they could commune directly with God, staring into His iris above the distractions of everyday life.

And so it was here where He turned to them to speak with the rhythmic beauty of the Realized Christ. "This is what I told you while I was still with you, 'Everything must be fulfilled that is written about Me in the Law of Moses, the Prophets and Psalms. It was written that the Christ will suffer and rise from the dead on the third day, and repentance and forgiveness of sins will be preached in His name to all nations, beginning in Jerusalem.'" He looked in the direction of the yawning city as it lay in the valley below. "I ask that you not leave the City of Jerusalem, but wait for the promise of My Father, which you have heard from Me. For John truly baptized with water, but you shall be baptized with the Holy Spirit not many days from now."

The Eleven sat riveted to these words, but still asked the question that had been on their tongues since He first appeared to them so many Sundays before. It was James who stood to ask Him, "Lord, will You at this time restore the kingdom to Israel?"

The Risen Christ answered, "It is not for you to know the times or seasons which the Father has put in His own authority. But, you shall receive power when the Holy Spirit has come upon you, and you shall be witnesses to Me in Jerusalem, and in all Judea and Samaria, and to the end of the Earth." And then He raised His hands prayerfully open to His Father and blessed them with the very words of His Abba, given so many years ago by God to Moses. "The Lord bless you and protect you. The Lord make His face to shine upon you, and be gracious to you, and look with favor upon you and give you peace." And when He had spoken these things, He began to ascend slowly upward and into a billowing, white cloud that had come to the summit. Gloriously, lovingly, He was taken up until they could no longer see Him in the white thickness of the cloud. The Eleven arched their necks and moved to better vantage points to find Him. They looked deeply into the swirling mist to search for one more glimpse of their Lord. They looked so deeply that they did not notice two men, dressed in glowing white robes, which stood by them and spoke to them in authority.

"Men of Galilee," one exclaimed, "why do you stand gazing up into Heaven? This same Jesus, who was taken up from you into Heaven, will so come in the manner as you saw Him go into Heaven." They were startled by these men, but understood the wisdom of their spoken words. In His ascension, Jesus was going home to sit at the right hand of His Father. And He would come back again by returning to this holy place just as He ascended. This time, they knew it was so. Still, they were astonished by the way they felt after seeing their Master depart. Once, just forty days previous, they were trembling and terrified in ignorance of His promised resurrection as He hung, beaten, on a cross. But now they were filled with a great joy in the understanding that the ancient prophecies had been fulfilled. The Lord had come, suffered, and died on a wooden cross, been resurrected back to His human breath and then ascended to sit at the right hand of His Father. The Messiah had brought them, not the earthly power that they thought they had desired, but the precious understanding of the true Kingdom of God. Each of them knew in his heart that they would return to Jerusalem to wait for the promise of the Father and then begin the commission, which the Christ had bestowed upon them this day on that high perch near Heaven. They would call out the Messiah's name to the ends of the known earth.

So Peter gathered them up as their leader and led them down the road back to Jerusalem. They tread lightly across the broken stones, like young children at play, until they entered the Northeastern Gate of the capital with singing hearts hardly silenced by the worn fabric of their robes. And on that day, and in the days to come, they were seen, always, at the Temple, praying and singing blessings to the Lord for the whole of each day, before returning home to the Upper Room in the evenings to await the promised gift of the Father. The Helper, the Counselor, the Spirit of Truth was coming to dwell inside each of them to guide them in their commission. The Eleven would be rested and ready to receive the promised gift with full faith. For now, they believed.

Saul strode back and forth across the tiled floor of his dining room while the light from a single, diminishing candle threw his shadow in monstrous size to dance upon the limestone walls. To see himself as a giant would have normally humored the bowlegged bantam, but he was immersed deep in his thoughts and hardly noticed the laughable discrepancy. The Pharisee was struggling with a problem in his mind that he intended to solve. And it would need to be solved, without question, before the expected return of the Galilean sect of the dead, but dangerous, Nazarene for the coming Feast of the Weeks. Saul had a gift for going straight to the heart of a problem, by focusing solely on the essentials and throwing away the distracting assumptions that often hung from the truth like baby lambs suckling their mother for milk. In his world, one was right or wrong; and to be wrong in the eyes of the Law of Moses could not be tolerated. Perhaps others were more flexible or more likely to adopt a wait and see attitude, but Saul knew that his appointment by the High Priest, Caiaphas, and his father-in-law, Annas, to destroy that sect before it took even a toddler's first unstable step, had been determined by their understanding of his zeal to protect the Law. He had been circumcised, according to the Law, on his eighth day, as a member of the tribe of Benjamin. He was a Hebrew born of Hebrews as to the Law of a Pharisee. There would be a winner, and a loser, here in Jerusalem, without even a single sliver of wood to serve as the first balustrade of a fence upon which the unsure could sit and wait to see.

The Law, as always, would be the final judge, like the confident surety of Solomon who once presided over the people of Israel with his judicious wisdom. And in Saul's contemplation of that problem, he would seek not only a solution, but also an opportunity to capture the Galileans in the folly of their own misunderstandings.

The northern wall of his flickering room stopped him, so Saul swirled about to walk in the other direction like a father banished to the anteroom of his own son's delivery by a stout midwife of few words. "Ah, the solution cannot be blended into weakness," he thought to himself. "I learned at Gamaliel's feet, and with all of the Rabbis of the Temple, that the Messiah was a savior of the future. This time in history was to be dedicated to the absolute obedience to the Law of Moses. If the people of Israel were diligent and fulfilled their destiny, then the stage would be set for the arrival of the Messiah—a savior who would come with a salvation defined and promised by the Law. Yes, then the true Messiah would inaugurate a new age, a glorious new age in which the Law would no longer be needed. He would destroy the sinners and drive out the Gentiles so that the chosen people, the twelve tribes of Israel, could ascend into a Messianic community free from sin. Blameless, purified, deserving, completed. But the Messiah could not, would not, arrive until the people of Israel consummated their obedience to the Law, without question, so as to construct the very door for the Messiah to enter. History could not overlap. And yet, these crazy Galileans, bamboozled by the soothing words and clever tricks of the Nazarene, were secretly going about Jerusalem, and surely in Galilee, claiming that the Messiah had come in the form of that itinerant Rabbi Jesus.

I have my spies—they hear more than the Galileans would imagine, as they hide in the home of the merchant. How foolish, how wrong! The proof could be determined by a simple walk about the city amongst the sinners who fall far short of their obedience to the Law with their shallow ways and decadent desires. No Messiah could come to save a people who were not ready for their salvation. This sect is a direct threat to the Law—how can one not see this as clearly as the hand I hold up in front of my face? Believe in Jesus and you reject the Law. Believe in the Law and you must reject this Jesus."

A loud rap upon his front door startled Saul from his studied contemplation. With some irritation, he changed directions to walk toward the annoying sound of the slapped wood. When he reached the front door, he sullenly called out, "Who is it?"

"It is Jacob, with my brother Isaac. We have news for you, Saul." The brothers were trusted members of the Temple police. A smile creased across Saul's face as he prepared to open the door. No two brothers in all of Israel were more different than Jacob and Isaac. The older, Jacob, was a tall, angular man with a pointed face pulled down by a thin beard that hung down past his chest. His eyes drooped like teardrops under bushy, black curved brows and constantly darted around like a cornered jackal. His brother, Isaac, was plump and short with springy hair that circled his head, but fell no further than his ears, which stuck out from his rounded crown like a surprised mule. And their body types were perfectly suited to their profession. No crowd could keep Jacob in ignorance, as he viewed their conversations and communal gatherings like a keen eyed hawk from above. Then there was Isaac, who could hear a snake slithering on a wet cave floor in perfect alacrity from two stone throws away. They constantly argued with each other over their findings, but their harsh words sharpened their witness to high reliability. In the end, they saw, they listened—and then always came by agreement to Saul, to spill the secrets of the people. They were worth their weight in gold or silver, these two; and Saul opened the door with a flourish to greet them.

"Gentlemen, please come in. I am delighted to see you two. And even more to see you not bickering!" exclaimed a smiling

Saul. "Please come in and enjoy a goblet of some fine wine. For what do I have the pleasure of this visit?"

As was generally the case, Isaac spoke first. "Good evening to you, too, my lord. I am afraid our professional duties will keep us from accepting your offer for a pleasing drink. We have important news to tell you."

"Pray, go on then," said Saul.

The prickly voice of Jacob tumbled downward to Saul from above like summer hail. "The men from Galilee have returned to the home of the merchant who lives in the Upper City. I have seen them with my own eyes."

"And I have heard them, singing and blessing God in the Temple like young students full of mirth," cried out Isaac, as his fleshy jowls quivered in concert. "They do not speak of the Nazarene, but are calling out to the Almighty with constant song and praise."

Saul blanched in surprise. "You do not hear them speak of this Jesus? Have they forsaken their poor Messiah, come to their senses?"

The brothers shook their heads no in unison. "They arrived yesterday, before dusk. We waited to observe their actions today before coming to you with our report," said Jacob.

"We should return to our posts to see if we can hear more," said the rotund Isaac, as his taller brother nodded his agreement.

"Yes, of course," Saul agreed, "but stay in close touch with me. I want to set a trap for these uncouth men. They haven't the education, or the cunning nature, to see this one coming." The two brothers shared the same laugh. How strange was it that their mother and father gave them a hundred different features that only merged at the exact point of their expressed joy? "So keep them in sight and well within the sounds of those ears, Isaac," Saul continued, "for it is time to increase the pressure on these unfortunate souls. Perhaps I will challenge them to recite one of our most cherished prayers. If they do so, I will point out the contradiction of their words to pray for a salvation when they claim the One who will bring this new age of glory has already come. And, if they choose not to pray the prayer, then I will accuse them of falsity, or even blasphemy, should they mimic the words spoken by their departed Rabbi. Either answer and I will pull the ropes of a snare about their foolish beliefs and expose them to all who live by the Law in our Temple."

"I shall keep my eyes open for every gesture, every meeting," promised Jacob, his eyes seeking shade under the portico of his knitted brow.

"And I shall hear every word whispered in confidence, if I am within distance," said Isaac, as he twitched like a horse hearing thunder in an open field.

Saul bowed respectfully to the two brothers and thanked them for their commitment. The brothers took their leave to return to the Temple. Saul was to eat supper that evening at the invitation of Caiaphas, and would surely pass on that very interesting information to the High Priest. "The visit by the brothers will make for an entertaining story at dinner," he gloated to himself, "It's good to have such talented men like Jacob and Isaac on my side of the Law. The lot from Galilee will walk, soon enough, into one of my snares and entangle themselves in a noose of their own making. We'll see if they are so full of mirth when they are dangling helplessly in the air. We'll see if their laughter can be heard over the unmistakable sound of a whistling stone cracking open a lawless skull."

There was a noisy bit of jostling in the Upper Room, as one hundred and twenty Galileans scrambled and nudged their way into position to hear Peter speak. The broad shouldered leader, a far cry from the beaten and contrite man of just six weeks previous, stood as still as a polished statue, while waiting for everyone to settle into place. Mary, the mother of Jesus, was seated just to his right, in close proximity to John, and next to Jesus' younger brothers, Jose, Simon, Judas and James, who had spoken privately with the Risen Christ a fortnight ago. The four brothers, forever disbelievers in the Rabbi as He went about His wandering ministry, were now as committed to Him as they were once embarrassed by His provocative acts and fanciful parables. James was rising in leadership, and his eyes shined with faith and devoutness. Lazarus of Bethany sat quietly in waiting, with Martha and the Magdalene, Joanna, Salome, and both, Cleopas and his wife, Mary. The Eleven reclined in a tight circle around their leader's confident stance. A look about the room confirmed that almost every one was there that had been with the Twelve, and Jesus, since His baptism in the desert by the wild eyed John the Baptist. Everyone was here, with the obvious exception of Judas the Betrayer. The Resurrection had changed everything. The Galileans in the Upper Room that day, now understood that the parables and the narrative, the supernatural acts, and the signs of Jesus fit perfectly into a prophesied pattern that had been passed on from family to family in the telling and retelling of a single story around burning fires for centuries. Now, the great middle of the story had come and gone. The Scriptures were alive, and every sentence spoken in the Word was fresh with the new meaning. The Galileans, these followers of the Way, had fallen into fervent, constant prayer without a separation of men and women. Everyone was of one accord in prayer and supplication. Everyone acted together in praise and worship. And in the center of the room sat Eleven men—not one of them formally educated, or from Jerusalem, or even presently employed—who had been commissioned by the Lord, Himself, to tell the story of the good news to the far corners of the Earth. By His request, they were waiting here in Jerusalem for the Gift of the Father to arrive as promised. And so, it naturally took a few moments for the hubbub to die down so that Peter could call the question on an unfinished piece of business.

"My brothers and sisters," he began in his booming Galilean accent, "this Scripture had to be fulfilled, which the Holy Spirit spoke before by the mouth of David, concerning Judas, who became a guide to those who arrested Jesus, for he was numbered with us and obtained a part in this ministry." A disagreeable rumble shook the room with enmity, but Peter silenced it with one wave of his hand. "Now Judas lies in the Field of Blood, for it is written in the Book of Psalms—'Let his dwelling place be desolate, and let no one live in it,'" said Peter in full confidence. "And, it is written, 'let another take his office.'" The one hundred and twenty now murmured in excitement, and some took to slapping their hands upon the floor. Someone was going to replace Judas and join the Eleven. Peter then began to specify the qualifications for the one who would become the twelfth apostle of the Lord Jesus Christ, by replacing the great betrayer. "Therefore, of these men, who have accompanied us all the time, that the Lord Jesus went in and out among us, beginning from the baptism of John, to that day in which he was taken up from us, yes, one of these must become a witness with us of His resurrection." Immediately, names were shouted out by those in attendance. Some were yelled out only once, and receiving no acclamation, fell harmlessly between the legs of the seated faithful. But others seemed to inspire a momentum, until at last only two names were heard above the din. Barsabas, surnamed Justus, and championed by the powerful proposal of James, His brother, and the other, Matthias.

And so they turned to Peter and asked, "Who shall it be, Barsabas or Matthias?" They both enjoyed strong support from their Galileans brothers.

Peter cleared his throat so that his words would be heard in full clarity. "You know the way we have always made these decisions. When we are torn between two, we cast lots to see the will of the Lord. The High Priest has a place for two rocks in his breastplate. One will outshine the other to signify the Will of the Lord—but we shall not seek the guilty Caiaphas' guidance for this appointment. No, we shall pray directly to the Lord with this prayer, so as not to show any favoritism to one or the other. Remember the proverb, the lot is cast into the lap, but its every decision is from the Lord."

So, led by Peter, they prayed and said, "You, O Lord, who know the hearts of all, show which of these two You have chosen to take part in this ministry and apostleship to which Judas, by transgression fell, that he might go to his own place." And so they placed the two names on separate stones into a jar and allowed John to shake it about until a single stone tumbled from the vessel. They all were faithful in knowing that the name that fell upon the ground would be determined not by chance, but chosen by the unseen hand of the Lord. One fell, bounced, spun once like a broken dreidel, and then revealed a name scrivened upon its face; Matthias.

So Peter went to kneel in front of Matthias to tell the humble man that he was now to be numbered among the disciples. Once again, they would become the Twelve, to numerically represent the twelve tribes of Israel. They would be whole again in the eyes of the Lord. A single tear found its way around Matthias's nose only to disappear into his beard. The honor of his election fought valiantly with his humility, and his emotions loosened. But Peter, seeing that, called the other eleven apostles around Matthias to offer him a prayer of acceptance. Watching, the whole of the congregation knelt down to pray in thanksgiving that the lot had once again discerned the Lord's will. Matthias would be the twelfth one, selected by the Lord through the instrument of His believers, to repair the breech that had been caused by Judas. For now, they would wait in faith until the Day of Pentecost, seven days hence, for the arrival of the Holy Spirit. And that they did, in joy, in song and prayer until the morning sun of that day came to illuminate the new world from high in the eastern sky. For their world had already changed and soon, the rest of the world would follow.

The morning of the Day of Pentecost began like all the other mornings. The men awakened with beckoning hungers, and the women joined some of the men to prepare the morning meal. Two fires burned in the hollowed out ovens of the Upper Room, and some sought the warmth of the fire to take the creak out of their sleepy limbs. Still others, like James the brother of Jesus, began that morning in prayer. As it was written in the ancient book of Leviticus, when God spoke to Moses, today was the day to offer the first fruits of your harvest to the Lord. Two wave loafs of two-tenths of an ephah of fine flour and baked with leaven. These are the first fruits to be given in humble gratitude to the Lord. But James the Devout, and the others, who only felt the morning rays of the sun upon their prostrate backs, had no wheat to offer, no harvest from which to pluck out their first fruits. Nonetheless, they had their faith and obedience. And so the very first prayers of that day were given in that spirit—prayers of gratitude to the Lord for the gift of His Son and for the Promise of the Father that was coming today. Just as the first fruits of the harvest linked their gratitude to the Lord, so too did the first prayers of that morning set these believers in rhythm to His will. As the third hour of that fine morning shone through the windows opened to the spring air, the Twelve were sitting in a circle in the very center of the Upper Room. The excited conversations of the throngs of visiting pilgrims could be heard in the streets below. The capital was hosting pilgrims for the

Pentecost from Jewish communities as far west as Italy and east to Babylonia. The Twelve looked upon Peter with expectation; for he would often speak to them at that time before they left to pray at the Temple. A hundred others gathered about them in a respectful hush. On that day they were, as they had been for ten days, of one accord. They had personally witnessed the One who had come as the Messiah, and then had been taken up into a cloud to sit at the right hand of His Father. The quietude of the room joined them together in a shared joy that did not need to be spoken to be felt. John stole a glance at the bearded Peter. The thick chested one named Petros by Jesus, was as still as the others with his black hair tousled in ten directions. Even his shoulders were at rest and his sinewy forearms rested in repose upon his thighs. The Magdalene stood erect against the wall beyond Peter's head, with the slightest hint of a contented smile gently pushing her checks up into fullness. He smiled at her but she did not notice his endearment. Mother Mary sat with Aunt Mary and Cleophas, surrounded by the four brothers of Jesus who in that moment, reminded John of their departed father, Joseph.

The grief that had racked Mother Mary had subsided, and she drew strength from experiencing the truth of her Son, the Risen Christ. John then regarded each of the Twelve, but to look at one was to look at any of the others. They were all still, content, and seeming to share the same breath. And Peter had not moved even a finger, so John settled into that breath and allowed the tension to drain from his face all the way down until he felt a tingling in his liberated feet. He breathed once more to taste the joy. And then, beyond the limits of the whole of their imaginations, something truly extraordinary happened. A great, rushing wind tore into the Upper Room, exploding through the open windows and the door at the top of the stairs, which flew open with a sharp crack. The wind circled the entire room, filling every corner with a pregnant fullness until it compressed with dizzying speed to settle upon the Twelve in a tight swirl. The others witnessed flames above the heads of the Twelve, neither attached to wood nor person. And then, a single tongue sat upon each of the Twelve, as if it was falling from the flames, and they began to speak in dialects and languages that were unrecognizable to their Galilean friends. The Holy Spirit roared into their throats and gave them utterance to languages that they had never spoken before. And then, as quickly as children, they descended the stairs and poured together into the street for the Upper Room was too small to hold the power of that Gift.

A bustling of pilgrims regarded them with great curiosity and confusion. How could these Galileans be speaking in tongues from every nation under heaven? Pilgrims from Parthia, Medes and Elam heard them speak of the wonderful works of God in the language of their homelands. Those from Mesopotamia, Judea and Cappadocia; from Pontus and Asia, Phrygia and Pamphylia, Egypt, Libya, Crete and Arabia; and even visitors from Rome were amazed and perplexed by the cacophony of dialects that spoke in authority to the greatness of God. The visiting pilgrims were moved by the beautiful words spoken in individual languages of their understanding, but could not grasp how the Galileans could speak in such unfamiliar prose.

A formally educated and perplexed man from faraway Asia called out in Greek, "How is it that we hear each, in the language of which we were born? Whatever could this mean?"

A surefooted pilgrim with a boisterous voice answered him for all to hear. "Why, they are full of new wine. They're drunk!"

Then Peter stood up in the midst of the Twelve and raised his voice so that all could hear. He spoke to the startled pilgrims, "Men of Judea and all who dwell in Jerusalem," he called out in given authority, "let this be known to you, and heed my words. For these are not drunk, as you suppose, since it is only the third hour of the day. But this is what was spoken by the prophet Joel:

'And it shall come to pass in the last days, says God, That I will pour out My spirit on all flesh; Your sons and daughters shall prophesy, Your young men shall see visions, Your old men shall dream dreams. And on My menservants and on My maidservants, I will pour out My Spirit in those days; And they shall prophesy. I will show wonders in heaven above And signs in the earth beneath: Blood and fire and vapor of smoke. The sun shall be turned into darkness, And the moon into blood, Before the coming of the great and awesome day of the Lord, And it shall come to pass That whoever calls on the name of the Lord Shall be saved.'"

Now the throng of passing pilgrims were rooted to the very spot upon which they stood with open mouths. Peter, already strong by nature and now empowered by the rushing wind and searing fire of the Holy Spirit, spoke again in a voice that could be heard for the full length of that street, before turning down into the meandering alleys that led into the shops and homes of those from Jerusalem. "Men of Israel, hear these words: Jesus of Nazareth, a Man attested to you by miracles, wonders, and signs which God did through Him in your midst, as you yourselves also know—Him! being delivered by the determined purpose, and foreknowledge of God, YOU have taken by lawless hands, have crucified, and put to death, who God raised up, having loosed the pains of death, because it was not possible that He should be held by it!" The listening congregation was astonished by these words, each hearing the exhortation in his own language. They looked upon the stout one who was shouting out in passion and saw the presence of the patriarch, David, in his challenging words. Fear and a sword slash to their consciences began to overwhelm them, but not a single one shouted out to Peter in opposition. Instead, they took steps to move closer together as others, hearing the power of these words from adjoining streets, pushed in to stand before Peter. Peter, seeing that, paused for a moment until the entire street was full, and even younger men could be seen hanging from perches and balconies to hear his words. He waited before unleashing a single sentence that both, indicted those within earshot, and gave them an understanding of the first step to their own salvation. "Therefore," he boomed, "let all the house of Israel know assuredly that God has made this Jesus, whom YOU crucified, both Lord and Christ!"

And when the men of Israel heard that, they felt the collective pain of their own responsibility in the Lord's crucifixion, and were cut to the red blood of their frightened hearts, deeply enough for one of their lot to cry out to Peter and the Twelve for the rest of them, "Men and brethren, what shall we do?" For each of them knew the truth that what was done could not be undone. And so they wondered what they could do to make amends, to make things right in the eyes of God and to avoid His retribution.

Peter saw their regret and spoke in a voice that could be heard all the way to the steps of the Holy Temple. With a compassion that had once been shown to him, he said unto them, "Repent, and let every one of you be baptized in the name of Jesus Christ for the remission of sins; and you shall receive the gift of the Holy Spirit. For the promise is to you and to your children, and to all who are afar off, as many as the Lord our God will call." And with that, and other exhortations, three thousand souls came forward on that morning to receive the Word, and to be baptized in the cool waters of the pool that held water for the inhabitants of the Upper City. One by one, they stepped into the pool to be immersed fully in water and the Word by the apostles who stood in the pool with the water reaching beyond their knees. And when there were too many to baptize by just the Twelve alone, those who had been baptized turned to their brethren and dunked them down into the water of their new life. This was the day that the Church of Jesus Christ began to take hold in the people of Israel, and the whole of the world, as the truth of His life and resurrection was passed from the Twelve, and their one hundred and twenty friends, to men and women from every nation of the earth. For when Peter preached the realized truth, faith and the Church were born and linked together.

These new followers of the Way returned in time to their countries to speak of that day in awe at the dinner tables of their relatives and friends. Although the grain and grapes were of different varieties in these faraway lands, the bread that was baked, and the wine that was fermented, were consumed in one way and held one message—the remembrance of the body and blood of the Lord Jesus Christ. Those who stayed in Jerusalem continued steadfastly in the doctrine and fellowship of the Apostles, in the breaking of bread and in prayers. They walked daily to the Temple to say their prayers and went at night into the homes of their fellow believers to participate in the sharing of food in gladness and simplicity of heart, in praise of God and in remembrance of the sacrifice made by Jesus. Others, seeing the peace and favor bestowed upon the followers of the Way and the happiness that they naturally expressed, were added to the Church daily as they came forward to be baptized in His name. The good news was spreading one by one on the dusty roads that led from Jerusalem. And still, their enemies waited in patience for a mistake, seething and scheming for the exact time to pounce upon the Twelve and bring them to trial before the Sanhedrin. A trial that was sure to end with a verdict of guilty and a penalty of death.

John gently reached out and touched the shoulder of the leader from behind, "Peter, are you ready?"

Peter slowly opened his eyes, that had been closed in private contemplation, and shook his head once to return to the sights and smells of those milling about in the Upper Room.

"Is it time? Has the ninth hour of the day come upon us so soon?"

John smiled at Peter and nodded his head to answer yes. "The others have already left for the Temple. I did not want to rouse you from your thoughts. What has kept you so quiet in the midst of this commotion?"

Peter did not answer him until they had closed the door that led to the street. He looked at John with eyes that seem larger, more vivid than usual, and quietly said, "I was thinking of our enemies—of Caiaphas and Annas and the young Pharisee, Saul of Tarsus, who Joseph of Arimathea has warned us is a viper ready to strike from hidden sands."

"Are you afraid of them, Peter?" asked John.

A soundless mirth rolled through the barrel chested Galilean like the trembles of a distant earthquake. As John looked upon his old friend, Peter replied, "What is fear after what we have witnessed, John? What can they do to us in this world that could deny us our blessings in the next one? Have we not already seen that death is but an open door to being with our Lord again?"

"I understand your words, Peter," said John, "but I must tell you, I do not want to die!"

Peter stopped in his tracks and turned to smile benevolently at his younger friend and thought to himself, "Look at him, so devout in his knowledge of the Word but still reaching for the truth from the safety of the riverbank. Come in, my little brother, and remember that we are covered by the Lord Jesus Christ. How can we forget the words that He said to us at our last supper together, just moments after He foresaw my own thrice denial? At that table, Jesus said, 'Most assuredly, I say to you, he who believes in Me, the works that I do he will do also; and greater works than these he will do, because I go to my Father—If you ask anything in My name, I will do it.'"

Then Peter said, "Fear not, John. We shall only die if that is His will."

As they approached the gate of the Temple, that the people called the Beautiful Gate, they came upon a man lame from his mother's womb who lay crookedly in a heap in the dust begging for alms. His limbs lay like cut sticks stacked haphazardly as the muscles that would have supported them had withered away to thin strands with no strength. With some effort, the lame man twisted his gnarled neck upon his brittle shoulders and, seeing the approach of John and Peter, called out to them for alms. Then Peter, seeing that, held John in place with the touch of one hand, and fixed his eyes upon the crippled man to say, "Look at us." The lame man shuffled in the dust to give Peter his full attention, for he was expecting to receive a coin from one who had taken the time to speak to him on their way to their Temple prayers. He fixed his eyes upon them and waited. The cripple grimaced in pain, for it took some effort to hold his head up at an angle where he could keep his eyes upon the two men. Then Peter said, while standing erectly above the beggar's bundle of twisted limbs, "Silver and gold I do not have, but what I do have, I give you: In the name of Jesus Christ of Nazareth, rise up and walk." And he reached down to take him by the hand to lift him from the dust. Immediately, the lame man's feet and ankle bones received enough strength to hold his weight upon them. With amazement, the man, who was crippled, leaped up to see if the received strength was so. Standing for the first time in his life, he took a step, and then a leap as he tore into the Temple in wonderment and in praise to God. Joyously, he was singing at the top of his voice.

The people in the Temple saw him walking and praising God and were astonished, for each of them had passed him tens of times as he had lain in a crumpled heap at the Beautiful Gate. They were amazed to see him leaping about and shouting out his praise for God in the fullness of his voice. "What had happened?" they wondered, as the lame man returned to the entrance, jumping sideways between two shocked members of the Temple Police, one tall, and one as stout as an old ox, to grab hold of Peter and John in gratitude as they entered the Temple. Neither Peter nor John showed a touch of astonishment upon their faces and purposefully walked with the healed man to Solomon's Porch, where they prayed daily and held court with the followers of the Way.

Everyone at the Temple saw that healing as a miracle, a direct sign from God, so they ran to Solomon's Porch in the hope of hearing Peter speak and explain how such a thing was possible; everyone, except the two members of the Temple Police who scurried out the Beautiful Gate to report the incident to their master. Peter waited until the clamor of the people diminished enough for him to be heard above the excited shouts and praises for what they had all witnessed.

John took hold of the healed man's hand and led him to a place among the Twelve who stood nearby in their customary support of their leader. Peter regarded the commotion with great patience and was pleased to see their friend, Joseph of Arimathea, in attendance with his fellow Sanhedrin councilor, Nicodemus. And behind Joseph were the Hellenists, led by the blond Stephen, as they collectively hurried to seek a place between the hundreds of men who were shouldering their way into position to listen to the Galilean's explanation of that miracle. Of course, everyone had heard stories of this Jesus of Nazareth and his signs and healings; but had that power now settled upon this simple man who stood before them?

When the flutter of a small bird's wings could be heard in the stilled air of the Holy Temple, Peter began. "Men of Israel, why do you marvel at this? Or why do you look so intently at us, as though by our own power or godliness we have made this man walk? The God of Abraham, Isaac and Jacob, the God of our fathers, glorified His Servant Jesus, whom you delivered up and denied in the presence of Pilate, when he was determined to let Him go. But you denied the Holy One and the Just, and asked for a murderer to be granted to you, and killed the Author of Life, whom God raised from the dead, of which we are witnesses." Peter's voice trumpeted these words to every cornice of the Temple, and his accusation hung in the air like the smell of rotten milk. "And His name, through faith in His name, has made this man strong, whom you see and know," Peter roared out, while pointing to the healed man standing and grinning in the midst of his men, "Ah yes, the faith which comes through Him has given him this perfect soundness in the presence of you all." But when Peter saw that not even a single voice rose up in opposition to his accusation, and when he saw the looks of contriteness that stared back at him from the faces of the congregated men, he softened. "Yet now, brethren, I know that you did it in ignorance, as did also your rulers. But those things, which God foretold by the mouth of all of His prophets, that the Christ would suffer, He has thus fulfilled. Repent therefore, and be converted, that your sins may be blotted out, so that times of refreshing may come from the presence of the Lord. To you first, God, having raised up His Servant Jesus, sent Him to bless you, in turning away every one of you from your iniquities." And when they heard these words, the congregated men understood that Peter was calling on each of them to receive this blessing from the Lord. The burly man's accusatory words were personal, cutting, and painful to even hear, much less to accept. For Peter was telling them the twelve tribes of Israel were God's chosen people, and as such, the first to experience the living example of the promised Messiah. And yet, even though they were all complicit in the murder of the One, the Lord God would offer them His forgiveness if they would repent from their sins and accept baptism in the Holy Spirit of the Risen Christ. Peter was asking each of them, individually, to look into their own heart and to make their own decision, for no one comes to the Christ but one by one.

As the men milled about in discussion or stood rooted in

place in deep thought, a group of Sadducee priests ascended onto Solomon's porch and surrounded Peter and John, before forcibly seizing them. Still, Peter did not panic but asked, "On what charges do you hold us?"

The leader of the Sadducees answered him abruptly, while laying his hands on Peter and pushing him toward the gate with the help of the others. John, too, was aggressively dragged in that direction, but remained mute. "It is forbidden to speak of the resurrection of the dead in this Temple. We are the leaders here, and we will not allow you to speak of things that openly challenge our beliefs and teachings," said the Sadducee priest, before barking out an angry order to the Captain of the Temple. "Take them—it is already evening. Put them in custody overnight and we will bring them before the Sanhedrin first thing in the morning." In a tight circle, so as to discourage any attempt by others to grab Peter and John from their grasp, the Sadducees and the Captain and his men soon had the two disciples out of the Temple and into the evening air.

The sky had darkened due to the hour, but Peter was still able to discern a short, authoritative man with long red curls smirking between an angular member of the Temple Police and an officer even smaller and thicker in stature. "So this is the viper, Saul," thought Peter. "Why he even looks like a serpent biding his time to strike his prey."

The powerful Peter ground his feet into the loose clay in front of Saul, which halted the procession. For a moment, he just stared into the eyes of the Pharisee to look for some goodness or mercy. Nothing. Saul only regarded him disdainfully before remarking, "Go on," to the Captain's men, and he soon disappeared from Peter's sight behind the mass of arms and chests of those who held Peter and John tightly.

Back in the Temple, the power of the spoken Word was lingering far after the one who had spoken it was taken away. For on that day, two thousand more men came to believe, and they poured into the streets of the capital to spread the news to the thousands of pilgrims who were camping in and around the Holy City for the Feast of the Weeks. Over and over again, they told the story of the lame man's healing, the miracle that they had witnessed with their own eyes. They told of the leaping, the singing, the offered praise to Almighty God and the passionate speech of the Galilean. And in the quiet of the evening, around the small fires that lit up the surrounding countryside even to the heights of Mount Olivet, they whispered one name in the ears of their sleeping children. "Jesus."

The morning chatter of greetings between the seventy members of the ruling elite and priests of Jerusalem ceased as the Head Priest, Caiaphas, climbed the terraces to take his seat as the Nasi, the President. His father-in-law, Annas, a former High Priest himself, sat to his right, and to his left sat the grey bearded Gamaliel, a brilliant Rabbi who was the most respected authority, according to the time honored traditions of Rabbinical Law. Everyone in attendance was aware of the miracle that had occurred in the Temple on the previous afternoon. There was a certain intellectual challenge in finding the proper punishment for those impetuous Galilean fishermen; after all, it was an indisputable fact that the healing had happened, and even witnessed by some of the men in that room. Who would speak to the proper tradition? The lame one who had been healed was well known to the regal members of the Sanhedrin; for over forty years he had been as much a fixture at the foot of the Beautiful Gate as the oil flamed lantern that illuminated that entrance into the Temple. The light of one had always shone upon the unfortunate soul of the other.

The Council waited in anticipation as the High Priest

vigorously cleared his throat with a gloved hand over his mouth to block the clearing spittle. "Bring them before us," boomed Caiaphas, as two members of the Temple Police hastened to the small holding room that held the accused before trial. Seventy-one sets of eyes followed the path of the two Galileans as they were led to the place before the Council. They were dressed in simple, peasant robes and unadorned by even the most modest of jewels or precious stones to show their standing or education. The two men were shuffled into place and stood stoically in front of the peering Sanhedrin. Still, they did not show fear nor the mercy seeking looks that many of the accused affected as their fate was called to question. The High Priest, Caiaphas, wasted no time in getting to the crux of the matter. "Simon bar Jonah, John bar Zebedee—this Council does not dispute that you healed the lame one who begs for alms at the foot of the Beautiful Gate yesterday afternoon." The High Priest fixed his gaze upon the two men and in an authoritative voice demanded, "but by what power or by what name have you done this?"

Peter did not respond to that question with words of defense, but spoke as an instrument of the Holy Spirit. A strong confidence spilled upon him and his prose, again, was that of a man far more formally educated in the nuances of the Law. Filled with the Holy Spirit, Peter spoke out to the seated Council, "Rulers of the people and elders of Israel. If we, this day, are judged by a good deed done to a helpless man, by what means has he been made well, let it be known to you all, and to all the people of Israel, that by the name of Jesus Christ of Nazareth, whom you crucified, whom God raised from the dead, by Him this man stands before you whole." All eyes turned to see the healed man, quietly praying as a witness in an offered chair before the Council. The Council, especially the Sadducees who sat in the greatest number, was astonished to hear that open declaration from that simple man—a declaration that ran counter to their most cherished beliefs, and directly threatened their earned position of power among the elite. But Peter did not notice their consternation and continued on with great clarity, "This is the stone which was rejected by your builders, which has become the chief stone. Nor is there salvation in any other, for there is no other name under heaven given among men by which we must be saved."

Without hesitation, Caiaphas, and the others, exploded in response to the perceived dauntlessness of those professorial statements from one who had only learned how to set a net into the sea in his upbringing. Quickly, Caiaphas motioned for the two Temple policemen to return Peter and John to the holding area out of sight and sound to the Council, and settled back into his chair to hear the responses from the astonished members. An angry Sadducee priest from the first row began the discussion. "It is clear that these two men are breaking the Law to call this Jesus the Messiah. We have not authorized this declaration—in fact; we were the ones who brought the blasphemous rabbi before Pilate for the sentence of death!" The statement was met with a chorus of affirmation from many sitting in attendance. "Did this man not accuse us of murder by saying whom YOU crucified? Did he not challenge our beliefs on the resurrection of the dead, by saying that his man was raised by God from his tomb! Preposterous! What should we do with these men?"

Still another wondered, "Such boldness from one who is uneducated and untrained in the ways of the Law. How could this be so?"

Nicodemus answered that query from his chair by saying, "They were with the Nazarene for three years before his death. Perhaps they were taught a basic understanding of the structure of the Law by the Rabbi." The rosy blush that colored his cheeks did not expose him to the others. Only Joseph of Arimathea knew his secret—that he, too, had been instructed by Jesus on the Law and was present at his burial. The secret was safe with Joseph. The respected merchant would not speak, for he was still suspected of being in collusion with the Galileans and, therefore, considered biased as to their sentencing.

Then Annas spoke from his seat of power. Although his appointment as the High Priest had been passed on to his son-in-law some years hence, the powerful patriarch of the Temple still wielded enormous political and intellectual wealth, and spent that capital wisely in a clever manner. He would often hear all sides of an argument before offering his opinion; an opinion that held within its words the experience of a man who had faced crises before and discovered solutions. Often, the members of the Sanhedrin waited upon his wisdom and were not surprised when Caiaphas ordered his wishes into law. He spoke without modulating his voice, logically and with understated eloquence. "Men of Israel, let us look at the facts of this matter. A notable miracle has transpired. We know this and thousands of pilgrims here in Jerusalem know this. It is evident that a truly miraculous healing came to pass yesterday—of this, we cannot deny." He waited to allow a murmur of affirmation to sweep across the Hall. "If we do deny this to the people, then they will rise up against this lie in insurrection; an insurrection that would be met with a swift, vicious judgment by the Romans. On the other hand, we cannot allow the telling of this miracle to spread to other nations. It must be stopped here. To allow the spread of this story is to infuriate the Romans who do not like to hear fantastical tales of a people's king. After all, there is but one Emperor." Again, he paused and heard no cries of disagreement. A silence seized the Hall, as the seated Sanhedrin waited for his guidance to that conundrum of what to do with the two men. Annas stood to drive his words home. "We cannot fulfill our chosen roles as instructors and protectors of our precious Law if we do not have the support of the Romans. They are simply too powerful. We will cease to exist, and the people of Israel will fall into sin and poverty without our guidance. Therefore, I propose," he said, while nodding in respect to the High Priest, "that we insist that this story spread no further among our people. Let us severely threaten these men, and their brethren, to never again speak to any man in this man's name—ever!"

There was such support for that conclusion that the High Priest, Caiaphas, called for the police to bring in the two Galileans from the holding room in the Hall of Hewn Stone without the taking of a ballot. Not a word was spoken, as the members of the Sanhedrin held their tongues, when Peter and John were placed in the center of the semi circle to face the decision of that Court. The two accused stood shoulder to shoulder and looked up to hear the words of Caiaphas. And the High Priest said, "A decision has been made. A binding decision that I know you will follow in full obedience. To not do so would be a very poor choice, and possibly a fatal one." Caiaphas stood in his ornate robe to deliver the sentence. Lines of fatigue creased his face and he was seething and gruff in his delivery. "You will not speak at all, nor teach in the name of this Jesus. If we hear one more word said in his name, then you will face the full fury of this Court. Will you comply with this order?"

It was John who answered the High Priest in clear voice, saying, "Whether it is right in the sight of God to listen to you more than to God, you judge. For we cannot but speak the things which we have seen and heard."

Caiaphas rapidly replied in a thunderous voice, "You may speak of whatever you have seen or heard. But—if you speak or teach in the name of this man, prepare for your death. It will not be tolerated. Now, get out of my sight before I change my mind. There are many men here who would rather see you dead than show you this mercy. Do not throw away this gift. Now, go. Go!" Again, seventy-one sets of eyes watched the two fishermen walk the length of the Hall to be released through the front door of the Hall into the Temple grounds. They were very fortunate to still possess their liberty; for the people believed in them, and were glorifying them in God's name for what had been done. Clearly, their execution could cause a riot in the streets—an ugly uprising of the commoners. Still, seventy one heads speculated as to which path the Galileans would choose as they were pushed through the massive entrance door and into the street—would they turn to walk in obedience with that decree or step in the direction of their own death?

Stephen approached the merchant's home on his way to the Upper Room. He was met by the Magdalene. "Are you coming to break bread again with us this evening?" she asked, as she observed the graceful Greek.

The blond curls of Stephen's closely cropped hair shimmered in delight as he greeted Mary. "Perhaps, my sweet friend, but I have a piece of business to discuss with Peter or John." He bowed respectfully to this reverent woman. "Are they upstairs?"

"Yes, they are. They want to speak to all of us tonight about what was said to them before the Sanhedrin this morning. Oh, Stephen, yesterday, did you see the healing of the lame man who sits at the Beautiful Gate?"

"I was not at the Temple to witness it, my friend. But nothing else but the miracle was being spoken about in the streets of Jerusalem today. Everyone is praising God for the miracle. And I saw the man this afternoon—still jumping about and singing his praises to the Lord," said Stephen, as he pantomimed the leaping of the healed man to Mary's obvious pleasure. Settling down, he followed the laughing Magdalene into the home and they climbed the stairs together up to the Upper Room.

The Upper Room was packed with almost every known

follower of the Way. Peter did acknowledge the entrance of Stephen and Mary, but did not smile at them. He was surrounded by the seated Twelve, save John, who stood just to his left shoulder. Stephen could see that Peter was as serious and focused as he had ever seen him. "Whatever he is going to say, will be very important," Stephen said to himself wordlessly. "I am fortunate to be here for this moment. So fortunate, in fact, that I cannot even remember the business that brought me here."

"My friends," Peter began, "It is known that John and I were called before the Sanhedrin this morning to answer questions on the healing of the lame man yesterday—the healing done through the faith this man had in our Lord Jesus Christ." The excited audience chirped their approval, but Peter raised a hand to halt their enthusiasm. He was not in the mood to be interrupted in saying what he wished to declare. Forthrightly, he went on, without a trace of bitterness or enmity in his voice. "The High Priest, Caiaphas, pronounced our sentence after they discussed our case, while we waited in a holding room. Of course, they could not deny the healing, for the man who was healed in Christ's name was with us in the Court. We broke no laws, so no punishment was administered. And yet," Peter bellowed with an inquisitive tone, "Caiaphas has commanded that we are not to speak nor teach a word in the name of our Lord Jesus Christ. Pray tell, what say you to that command?" Hundreds of no's cascaded down upon the stalwart speaker. Peter accepted their response, but moved them to a respectful silence when he lifted up his hands to pray. "Then raise your voice in one accord with me in this prayer. 'Lord, you are God, who made heaven and earth and the sea and all that is in them, who by the mouth of King David it was said—Why did the nations rage, and the people plot vain things?' The kings of the earth took their stand, and the rulers were gathered together against the Lord and against His Christ.'"

Stephen heard these words and moved closer into a position where he could better hear the spoken prayer of the sharpened leader. He wondered, "What has happened to this simple man? He speaks with the wisdom of the Rabbi of Rabbis, Gamaliel, and with such confident authority and prose. I understand what he is saying and praying—that the powers to be will always fight against the Lord and His Christ." He thought of Caiaphas and Annas and of that disagreeable zealot, Saul, who had threatened him on two occasions. "Yes, they will not give up their power—even to the Risen Christ."

And Peter went on, fervently praying, "Now, Lord, look on their threats, and grant to Your servants that with all boldness they may speak Your word, by stretching out Your hand to heal, and that signs and wonders may be done through the name of Your holy Servant Jesus."

Stephen was thrilled to hear these words resound in his ears and in his heart. "I understand, I truly do. Peter is emphatically asking for God's providence to us. To give to us by His hand, or in His plan, whatever must be done to survive the threats of the rulers, the kings of the earth? To give us boldness to witness and for renewed powers through the name of Jesus." And as the angelic Greek came to that understanding, the Upper Room began to shake with tremors and a fine, white dust began to fall from cracks in the limestone walls. The plates that held the food that would be shared in fellowship trembled and tinkled against the earthen cups, as the wine in them spilled over their tops and onto the table. Tall chairs lost their balance and tumbled to the wooden floor. The Holy Spirit descended upon each person in that room and took hold of them as they shouted out the Word of God in boldness. Even the meekest of them was compelled to witness, and they all glorified His name in a manner that would have seemed impossible before that prayer was spoken. Stephen, already charismatic and in a loving rhythm with God and His son, was struck numb by the Holy Spirit, which washed from him any vestiges of doubt that sought to cling to his faith like swollen leeches. Wave after wave of soul shaking spirit swept his body clean in the name of the Lord and he knelt to his knees. "I have been given the power of the Spirit from the Lord—a cleansed voice to speak boldly in the name of Jesus. Now I realize my destiny, for my time to witness to all in this world has come." And as Stephen humbly accepted his destiny in God's plan, he glanced about the room to see that all of the others were still visibly experiencing the power of the Holy Spirit's descent upon them, except for their leader, Peter the rock, who stood stoically at the very spot from where he had said that prayer. He was amazingly calm in the midst of the frenzied activity which swirled about him in every direction. Stephen was near enough to the restored leader to see just the hint of a smile of contentment come to his lips. A very slight upturning of the corners of his mouth that seemed to reveal what he knew in his heart. The prayer had been answered.

Through the weeks that followed the answered prayer for boldness, as the intermittent breeze of spring gave way to the searing heat of the summer sun, more signs and wonders were done through the hands of the Twelve, and all in His name. The stories of the healing of the lame man and what had happened during the Festival of Weeks began to spread to all nations as the pilgrims present at the Pentecost returned by caravan to their homes near and far. They carried their witness inside their robes until these stories were unpacked at the dinner tables of tens of thousands of foreign homes. Many of those who were baptized by the followers of the Way during the Festival did not leave Jerusalem, and all possessions were shared to buy food and shelter for those who had chosen to remain. The Twelve continued to pray daily in one accord at Solomon's Portico and were joined by the passionate new followers, while still others stayed away in fear over the threat of punishment if they were to be seen worshipping with the apostles. Daily, new believers repented of their sins and were baptized by the apostles in the many pools near the Temple. Weekly, their numbers grew, despite being under the suspicious eyes of Saul and his minions, on order from the Sanhedrin. Even the inhabitants of the surrounding villages came into Jerusalem in great numbers, carrying their sick and afflicted, to lie on beds and couches in the streets near the Temple, in the hope that Peter would pass by and heal them when his shadow passed over their affliction. These superstitious villagers were not followers of Jesus, but believed that Peter possessed a healing magic borne of his own hand. Still, despite their ignorance as to the true source of that gift, many were healed.

Even the Pharisee, Saul, might have looked the other way for a bit of time, had not the Twelve been so publicly expressive as to in whose name they healed. The people were listening attentively and their popularity rose with every healing and every speech. The brothers, Jacob and Isaac, reported new transgressions daily to Saul, of the invoking of Jesus' name in both their interactions with the maimed and broken bodies and in their soaring prayers of gratitude. Saul wondered in amazement, "How can they break the Law so openly in full view of the entire community? How can they defy a direct order from the High Priest, the most powerful man, save Procurator Pilate, in all of Jerusalem? Enough is enough! I must go, this very morning, to the Temple and recommend to Caiaphas that we rearrest these Galileans and charge them with defying a Holy Decree. Are we not a people of the Law and what are we if we cannot enforce the Law? Such open disrespect cannot be tolerated! How can this still be a problem to us? What unseen force is aiding these foolish men and saving them from their deserved floggings?" So Saul called upon the two brothers, Jacob and Isaac, and gathered them for the walk to the Temple. "I might need their witness to convince the High Priest that the time to act is now," he thought. They were quite a sight as they made their way down through the throngs of those who lay in torn couches and wet beds in the street in front of the Temple—three men, one towering above the afflicted, and two others, one rotund and one gingerly stepping amongst the unclean so as not to debase his purity. Their progress was slow, as they often circled around a particularly tragic case, and gave great leeway to those who seemed possessed by the spirit of madness.

Nonetheless, as they neared the main gate entrance to the Holy Temple, a boil covered man, tormented by an unclean spirit which caused him to shake violently and spit in every direction, ran upon the horrified Saul and reached out to take hold of his robe. "Sir," the man cried out between shakes and random sprays of his brown spit, "have you seen Peter, the one who can heal me? Please, sir, can you tell me where I can find this holy man? I beg you."

"Let go of me this instant!" Saul screamed, but he would not have garnered his freedom had not the heavy boot of Jacob's foot crashed against the side of the man's head. But as the unfortunate man fell back onto the street in a fresh pool of his own blood, two other afflicted souls, one male and one female, surrounded Saul to ask the very same question.

Saul raised his right hand to strike one of them when he was interrupted by an authoritative voice loudly calling out his name. "Saul," snarled the High Priest himself as he stood at the great gate of the Temple, surrounded by a group of Sadducee priests and the Captain of the Temple Police with many of his men, "I have seen enough." A contingent of police tore off the filthy hands that clung to Saul, and cleared the whole area with a practiced violence. Regaining his dignity in the midst of his uncleanliness, Saul turned to face the High Priest. "I have instructed the Captain to take a contingent of men to arrest these Galileans. They cannot defy my direct order on behalf of the Sanhedrin, and live to tell the story," said the infuriated Caiaphas. He turned to the Captain to issue an order, "Take Jacob and Isaac with you. They know every face of the Twelve. I want them thrown into the common prison for this evening and then to appear before the whole of the Sanhedrin in the morning. Let them heal the rats, tonight, that sit in the wet pools of the dungeon. Go now and arrest them!"

Jacob and Isaac stopped their attempts to clean up and mollify Saul and fell into line with the departing policemen.

"And another thing, Saul," intoned the High Priest in sharp tones, "we must deal with the Greek, Stephen. There are reports that he is performing signs and miracles like our former friend. I have no patience for another magician! None, whatsoever."

"I shall look into that matter immediately," said the distracted Pharisee. When he was satisfied that he had cleaned the brown spittle from the diseased man from his robe, Saul took a step to enter the Temple.

"I think it is best if you seek a ritual cleansing, my friend," whispered Caiaphas. "You have been defiled and made unclean by this rabble. Until you do so, we cannot welcome you into the Holy Temple."

A tremendous anger rose up in a furious Saul, despite knowing that the High Priest was speaking in absolute accordance with the Law. "Of course, my lord, but hear my vow. Someone will pay for this indignity! Someone will pay for this insult to my family and my purity." The High Priest nodded his accord before turning to recommence his duties inside the Temple. He turned too quickly to hear the last three words spit out by the incensed Pharisee, in much the same manner as those spoken earlier in terror by the boil covered man. "With his life!"

ohn's eyes slowly adjusted to the inky darkness as the Twelve tried to sleep through the night on the cold, wet stones of the dungeon floor in the public prison. His fellow brethren were huddled together in small groups trying to stay warm, except for Peter, who was sleeping soundly in a sitting position up against the far wall. John could not sleep. The young disciple laid his head down upon an uneven sill of an iron barred window that opened to a hall, where a sliver of the morning light might be seen at dawn through a crack in a door that led out to the street. Peering out, he watched the rodents splashing through sitting waters before spraying the moisture from their pelts in shivering shakes. "How foolish," he thought, "just as they are dry, they leap back into the wetness. Look at them—they are just like us, saturating themselves in sin and struggling to shake it off before plunging right back into the puddled filth. And who will cleanse them?" In pain, John twisted his neck in a circle to get some relief from a cramping before laying his head back down upon the icy sill. Only two sounds permeated the dank murkiness, the scurrying about of the water soaked rats and the contented snoring of the fearless Peter; an act seemingly oblivious to the reality of their plight. So John focused on those two sounds to allay his fear and found some relief in the playful banter of the rodents set against the soothing cadence of Peter's snores. And as the night approached the dawn, and even the rats fell into a drowsy slumber, a small light appeared in the center of the largest puddle in the hall outside their cell. John blinked to see it and twisted his head to look up through the bars to find the source of that illumination. When his eyes returned to the puddle, the light had grown in circular size and shimmered on the very surface of the water. He watched in amazement, perplexed, and a bit frightened—frightened enough, in fact, to roughly wake up his brother, James, with a swift kick to his older sibling's curved back. "James, wake up. Look, there is a light shining in the hall and yet it is still night. Look, there—do you see it?"

James grunted in anger over being awakened, but did as his younger brother requested. On his knees, he looked sideways out of the iron barred window and saw the light shimmering in the puddle. "Yes, I see it," he answered, "it is just a reflection. Go back to sleep."

But just as James spoke his final word, the outer room exploded in a light too blinding to view. The locked door of the cell flew open with a loud bang, which awakened them all; and the powerful light came into the cell. The Twelve could do nothing but shield their eyes and look downward to avoid the incandescent rays. John tried to say something, but the fear of the moment seized his throat and not even a word could find its way to expression. A captivating voice called out, "Go, stand in the Temple and speak to the people all the words of this life." And then as quickly as the light had come, it extinguished. The men rubbed their eyes to refocus and peered out from between their fingers. "Who had spoken to them? Was it man or angel who had come in this blinding light?" they thought among themselves.

They wondered about in a puzzled state until Thomas cried out what he noticed, "The door is open! Look, the latch has been moved to one side." The normally frowning disciple picked up a twisted chain that had fallen to the floor and, with a grin upon his face, brought it over to Peter. The leader pulled it taut once in his hands and then rose to his feet. Without a word, he tossed the twisted chain to a corner of the cell and strode through the open door, before splashing through the filthy puddles. His men followed. Even the rats sat on their haunches and watched the Twelve leave that prison, their pink eyes reflecting the first rays of morning and their tails still twitching in a primal remembrance of the great light.

Even as the Twelve walked without interruption to Solomon's Portico to resume their teachings, the seventy-one members of the Sanhedrin were awakening to hear their case at the Hall of the Hewn Rock. The High Priest, Caiaphas, was already in his exalted seat when many members began to arrive before the third hour of the day. They greeted each other in solemnity, for they knew the seriousness of the pending charges. To defy a determined order of the Sanhedrin, which had been officially authorized by the High Priest in that very court, was a traitorous act. Traitors to the Law! The penalty? Death! "Good morning, gentlemen. I have sent the Captain of the Temple Police to the public prison to bring the Galileans before us today. I find their rebellious acts of defiance a threat to our very power. After all, we are only as strong as we are capable of punishing those who defy our orders." A low murmur filled the room and there was much nodding of the heads and statements of agreement made between the members before the formal proceedings would begin.

The room came to silence as the Captain and his men walked in without the company of the accused Twelve. The Captain gazed dumbfounded at the assembled congregation. Caiaphas spoke assertively, "Captain, where are the ones I sent you for?"

The Captain hesitated before answering in a plaintive voice, "We went to the prison, but found the door to their cell locked. When we opened the door, there was no one inside!"

"Captain, that is impossible!" thundered Caiaphas. "I command you to go right back to the prison and bring me those men, unless you want to take their place in the cell."

But just as the High Priest was issuing that command, a late arriving Pharisee member spoke out before he took his seat on the second row of twenty-three. "The men from Galilee are preaching at Solomon's Portico. I saw them with my own eyes on my way here."

Again, Caiaphas exploded with anger, saying, "But that is impossible. If I find out one of our men is responsible, then I will ask Pilate, himself, for the right to stone him to death. And I will throw the first stone!" No one in attendance had ever seen the High Priest that angry. Even his powerful father-in-law, Annas, sat demurely in his seat, uninterested in trying to calm his stormy son-in-law. Caiaphas regarded the Captain with disdain and changed his order in light of the new information, "Bring them back to us from Solomon's Portico. Be very careful, Captain, they have great popularity among the people, so do it without causing a commotion. NOW!"

Within the hour, the Captain and his men, alongside Saul with Jacob and Isaac in tow, entered into the hall with the unbound, but compliant Twelve. The Temple police placed the men in the customary area where the accused always stood to face the Sanhedrin. Doing that, they left quickly, as did Jacob and Isaac, but Saul remained in the Hall and took a seat near one of the clerks. He would not be able to speak or address the Twelve unless called to witness, but he would be allowed to listen to the accusation and the decision rendered by the ruling elite. When everyone was settled and ready, Caiaphas began, "You have been brought before the Sanhedrin to answer to the accusation of your rebellious defiance of an official decree. Did we not strictly command you not to teach in this name? And look, you have filled Jerusalem with your doctrine, and you intend to bring this man's blood upon us!"

Peter took one step forward to signify that he would speak for the others. There was no trace of fear or anger in his being as he began to answer the charge. With great courage, he replied, "We ought to obey God rather than men. The God of our fathers raised up Jesus whom you murdered by hanging on a tree. Him, who God has exalted to His right hand to be Prince and Savior, to give repentance to Israel and the forgiveness of sins. And we are His witnesses to these things, and so also is the Holy Spirit, whom God has given to those who obey Him."

The Hall ruptured into an unrestrained chaos. These powerful men, who considered themselves deeply pious, and both teachers and judges of the Holy Law, could not, would not, accept even an accusation of murder! Despite Caiaphas's pleas for order, the men screamed out their fury at Peter and the Twelve, and multiple schemes to kill them rang out throughout the Hall in fits of rage and fist shaking. So egregious was that accusation, that the Twelve might have been illegally murdered on the spot had not an eminent voice of reason been heard above the hateful din. It was the temperate voice of the Rabban, the one who had been given the honored title as the teacher of the Rabbis, Gamaliel. Out of respect to his scholarship and his sweeping understanding of even the most obtuse traditions of the Law, the furious members corralled their hatred into their pounding chests and gave the Rabban the silence that he needed to be heard. The aged Rabban stood up to address his brethren, a bit unsteadily, but a Sadducee priest to his left supported him with his own right arm.

"With all due respect, High Priest, Caiaphas," said Rabbi Gamaliel, "may we speak in private session." Caiaphas agreed immediately and the Twelve were led to the waiting room where Peter and John had been detained a fortnight ago. Rabbi Gamaliel thanked the High Priest and spoke privately to the one who was assisting him, who returned unobtrusively to his seat. With a clarity that belied his age, he began to say in measured tone, "Men of Israel, take heed to yourselves what you intend to do regarding these men. For some time ago, Theudas rose up, claiming to be somebody, a Messiah. A number of men, about four hundred, joined him. He was slain, and all who obeyed him were dispersed. After this, Judas of Galilee rose up in the days of the census, and drew away many people after him. He also perished, and all who obeyed him were dispersed." The Rabban's eyes were afire with wisdom, and the men in attendance waited in anticipation for his lesson. It always came, unadorned and naked in its simplicity. The old teacher raised his gnarled, right hand to drive home his words, and spoke with the passion of a younger man when he said, "And now I say to you, keep away from these men and let them alone; for if this plan, or this work is of men, it will come to nothing—but if it is of God, you cannot overthrow it—lest you even be found to fight against God!"

The members of the Sanhedrin considered the clearheaded logic and wisdom of Rabbi Gamaliel's well spoken words. As usual, the Rabban had struck to the heart of the matter and sought to find a divine solution. His answers were always clever in construction, and forever respectful of God's sovereign hand in history. A brief discussion ensued, but the balanced plan of the Rabban was approved by acclamation. The High Priest, Caiaphas, acknowledged that concordance and motioned to the remaining guards to bring back the Twelve for sentencing. "Galileans," Caiaphas intoned, "a wise Rabbi has convinced us of our divine direction. You are fortunate that we have decided to spare your lives. But I would temper your rejoicing—if you continue to speak in the name of Jesus, then we will have no other alternative but to meet your defiance with the most severe of measures. Now for this offense—your direct disobedience of an official decree of the Sanhedrin—I sentence you to forty lashes, save one. I pray that the sting of each lash that tears into your back brings you a greater understanding of our seriousness." The High Priest rose to his full height and commanded the returning Captain to commence the whipping immediately. "Whip them in the courtyard of this Hall, Captain. I don't want to make a spectacle of their punishment in front of the people. I am convinced that these men will come to understand the errors of their ways. We can coexist under God's guidance. We ask only that they cease to teach in this man's name. Whip them here, where we can hear them come to this understanding."

And so the Twelve were led out into the courtyard adjacent

to the Hall of the Hewn Rock, where they were lashed thirty nine times each. Not a one of them cried out for mercy or wailed in painful agony. Yes, the congregated members of the Sanhedrin could hear each crack of the whip and the natural grunts of acceptance, but they could neither hear nor see what beat in the hearts of these men as they endured the shameful beating. They considered it a joy to be counted worthy of suffering in His name, linking themselves to the shared agony of their beloved Lord. A joy to know that these whips could not touch the peace permeating their beings nor hinder the assignment that had been given to them by Jesus before He had ascended into the clouds above.

On that night, the Twelve apostles were tended to in the Upper Room by the women, who tore strips of linen soaked in warm waters to cleanse their wounds. It was close to midnight when they finally went to rest, sleeping on their stomachs as the woman applied homemade ointments to the gashes in their backs. And yet, still they awakened early on the next morning and walked briskly to the Temple, to their preaching perch at Solomon's Portico. Once there, they did not cease to teach or proclaim the one truth that they now knew they had been hand selected to trumpet unto probable death—Jesus as the Christ!

The charismatic Stephen was arguing with a throng of men at the Synagogue of the Freedmen. "Have you forgotten what the Lord said to His prophet Isaiah?" he questioned. "I tell you that the heart of the Lord lives in the heart of those who tremble at His Word, and not in those who have become too proud of their positions in the Temple and selfish in their privileges. Look at our people's history to see that we have always been too hard of heart and disobedient—when will we learn to be humble, to kneel in obedience before our Lord no matter where we stand?"

A Cyrenian challenged the handsome Greek as quickly as lightning strikes. "Are you saying the Lord does not rest in our Holy Temple? How dare you claim that the Lord has no need for His Temple." A chorus of voices agreed with that man, and their shouts caused Stephen to pause before he responded in unassailable debate.

"Thus said the Lord, as heard by Isaiah, 'Heaven is my throne, and the earth is my footstool,'" countered the clever Stephen, who often frustrated his opponents with his keen knowledge of the Word and faultless arguments. "What place on this Earth could possibly hold all of the glory of our God?"

An incensed man from Alexandria shook his fist at the Greek and cried out, "But it was King David who wanted to give our Lord a Temple, a place for Him to dwell forever. And his son Solomon built it magnificently and the Lord blessed it by filling it with His Shekinah glory, a holy demonstration of His divine presence."

Again, an uproar of harsh voices rose in approval of that challenge, and some of the men muttered vile oaths against Stephen within the safety of the din. Stephen, as always, chose not the path of anger, but allowed a smile to pleat his perfect features.

It had been months since he had been filled with the Holy Spirit on that late afternoon when Peter prayed the prayer for boldness. Since that precious day, he had been guided by the Spirit to teach and preach with a deep clarity of faith, and his sermons were like precious hymns floating to the heavens. It was thought that the thumbprint of God could be seen upon his forehead. The Twelve, beset by complaints on the distribution of food for all of the followers of the Way, had honored him and six other Hellenist men of faith and good reputation, by laying their hands upon them to appoint them to administrate the business matters of the ever expanding followers of Jesus. A great many of the new believers were priests, humble and devout men, who lived obediently to the Lord and proclaimed that Jesus was the Christ. The good news of the resurrected life of Jesus was spreading, as the ruling Sanhedrin remained bound by Rabbi Gamaliel's counsel.

On that fateful day, Stephen was face to face with the sharpest representatives from five of the most influential synagogues in Jerusalem, but he was confident that he would prevail in that spiritual battle of wits. "After all," he smiled to himself, "what am I, but an open vessel to God to speak His words through my tongue? What am I, but an innocent child blessed with a pure voice by my Father?" So Stephen replied, "I do not dispute that what you say is true. Nonetheless, God does not live in the Temple. He cannot be contained in temples made by our hands—even the hands of the great King Solomon!" Perhaps it was that mention of King Solomon, or perhaps the men from the five synagogues had just finally reached the climax of their frustration that caused them to forgo any further verbal sparring as they leapt upon the speaking platform and surrounded the victorious Stephen.

They would seek to defeat him with charges of impiety since they could not best him in spirited debate, so they resorted to plots and violence. "Take him to the Sanhedrin," cried out the defeated Cyrenian, and that plan met with universal approval by the smoldering mob. And they took turns pushing him forward as they stumbled toward the Hall of Hewn Rock where the Sanhedrin would be in session. Still the smile did not leave Stephen's face, for God was always inside of him, and so, too, was the Lamb of Ages. There were a group of Temple policemen standing guard at the door of the Hall. The boisterous mob pushed Stephen right up to the steps and demanded an audience before the Sanhedrin. One of the policemen disappeared inside the heavy wooden door, but returned in short order to announce that they would be heard. A cheer went up between the men and they pushed the young preacher into the Hall and to the place for the accused to stand in full view of the Sanhedrin's three rows of judges.

They did not leave the chambers after releasing Stephen, but stood at the open end of the Hall to encourage the Cyrenian, who spoke first to the assembled Sanhedrin. "This man does not cease to speak blasphemous words against this holy place and the law," he bellowed bitterly, while pointing, with malice, at the perfectly still Stephen, "for we have heard him say that this Jesus of Nazareth will destroy this place and change the customs which Moses delivered to us." The council gazed steadfastly upon the accused and were stunned by his beauty, truly the face of an angel. The spiteful words of the accuser, and the shouted corroborations of the mob, hung in the charged air as the ruling elite simply stared at Stephen in stupefied awe.

Soon enough, though, the High Priest, Caiaphas, silenced the disorderly crowd with one piercing stare, and then turned to unleash the full power of his prominent office upon the standing Hellenist. "Are these things so?" asked the High Priest in clipped cadence. Stephen answered the charge in melodious voice, and began his defense by speaking of Abraham. Slowly, surely, confidently, he took the assembled rabbis and elite on a generational journey of the Israeli story. Repeatedly, he pressed his case that the leaders of Israel had always shown disobedience to the Lord, and had continually rejected the divinatory words of the prophets. And, although the assembled Sanhedrin were extraordinarily well schooled in their own history, they neither challenged his telling nor interrupted him with questions.

They merely sat back in their chairs and listened attentively as Stephen spoke, for they would not cut short a summary of their sacred history. His words were hypnotic, and they labored to free themselves from his hold upon their senses, to separate the way he spoke from the devastating accusations that hid just beneath the surface of his symphonic speech. Still, Stephen sensed that he would not receive a fair trial from these hardened men, and he slowly shifted his defense away from a lecture and toward a fitting conclusion that the coming of the Christ meant that a clean break from the old order must come to fruition. The coming of the Messiah had changed everything. "Look at these men," he thought, "I can see the impatience creeping upon their faces. Our salvation lies not in adherence to a set of rigid rules, but to a surrender of our earthly desires and the acceptance of the Christ into our hearts. Lord, empower me with the words to glorify You and to speak the truth of your Son. I give you my life." And with the power of the Holy Spirit coursing through his veins, Stephen gazed upon the assembled congregation, and the mob which circled behind him and declared, "You stiff-necked and uncircumcised in heart and ears! You always resist the Holy Spirit; as your fathers did, so do you. Which of the prophets did your fathers not persecute? And they killed those who foretold the coming of the Just One, of whom now you have become the betrayers and murderers, who have received the Law by the direction of angels, and have not kept it!" There was not a single man in the room who did not react with shock to the condemning words from Stephen. Some of them were cut to their very heart, while others spit out heinous threats or diatribes. But Stephen gazed beyond them, and beyond his death in the fullness of the Holy Spirit, to proclaim what he saw in the sky, "Look! I see the heavens opened and the Son of Man standing at the right hand of God!" When the men heard these words, they stopped their ears and cried out violently. Even some of the august members of the seated Sanhedrin joined the mob in surrounding Stephen and seizing him. The authoritative words of the High Priest seeking order fell upon deaf ears, as the mob half dragged and pulled Stephen, by his white robe and golden sash, out of the entrance door of the Hall and into the street. A larger man grabbed the fallen teacher by his light colored curls, while others beat their hands upon his recumbent body, as he was dragged through the dust. Not a single member of the Temple police dared to intervene. A sickened Rabbi Gamaliel watched with a horrified Joseph of Arimathea, from the steps of the Hall; and they both recalled the words of the Nazarene when he had faced these same accusers on the night before his death: "Nevertheless, I say to you, hereafter you will see the Son of Man sitting at the right hand of the Power, and coming on the clouds of heaven." Joseph held the Rabban upright with a strong hand, as the old man murmured prayers for God's intervention.

Within minutes, the murderous mob was at the Damascus Gate and on the road away from the Temple, leading to the city of the same name. Stephen was covered with an earthy dust, but still smiling, his dignity intact despite the attack. Two men yanked him to his feet and his hands were bound behind him. "Push him," the crowd insisted, and Stephen was led to a threatening cliff and pushed over face first, tumbling onto the ground. The beautiful man landed upon his face and upper shoulder and lay still for a moment. Then, against the hopes of the false witnesses, he rose to his feet and smiled at the bloodthirsty throng. He was so beautiful, still glowing in his faith and humble in his bearing. "Stone him," cried the crowd, and the first rock hit him square upon the forehead and dropped him to a kneeling position.

A hundred stones came crashing upon him from the sky, but Stephen weathered the blows and called out to God by saying, "Lord Jesus, receive my spirit." Then, in a lull between throws, he rose one final time to his feet and then fell back down upon his knees without another rock being thrown. In a loud voice that could be heard to the Damascus Gate, he cried out, with his face shining in ecstasy through rivulets of blood, "Lord, do not charge them with this sin." And when that was said, he died, as if falling asleep upon the rocky terrain. He died like the Master he loved, forgiving to his very end.

A strange hush came over the murderers. Each of them

knew that the act had been illegal, and punishment could be forthcoming from the Romans when they came to know the story. They had all witnessed Stephen's unyielding faith, and had seen him die in peace despite being pummeled by stones. They had all seen the whispered and spoken prayers upon his lips. And so, in fearful silence, they filed past Saul, who had observed the stoning in its entirety. Once there, they laid their garments at the feet of the zealous Pharisee. One by one, they acknowledged their part in the stoning, seeking his consent to the deed. After all, the man from Tarsus held Roman citizenship, and his witness would be credible in Pilate's court. The menacing Saul bowed his forehead slightly as each garment was laid before him in respect to his power. And when the last of the murderers had filed past him, Saul turned around to look back upon the Gate of Damascus, the entrance to Jerusalem. There, standing in the midst of the Temple police, stood the High Priest, Caiaphas, with a smirk upon his face. When his eyes met Saul's, he signaled his approval with a nodding of his head, chin to chest. And then he smiled, before turning abruptly around to return to the Temple in the company of the police.

Saul stood at his place with the garments before him, until a group of devout men, pious Jews of Judea, came for the body of the serene Stephen. Saul ignored them, and also Jacob and Isaac, who gathered the presented garments and bundled them into packs to be carried back into the city. His mind was on the shift that would certainly commence in the morrow. For the first time since the crucifixion of the Nazarene, a follower's blood had been shed unto death. A line had been drawn and crossed in the desert sand. A line now covered with a martyr's fresh blood. Still, Saul did not carry these worries back with him into the city as he walked beneath the Damascus Gate. He would soon have the power for which he had been waiting for weeks—the power to seek out and crush the followers of the Way in one fell swoop—the power to eradicate the followers, like so many city rats, rousting them from their hidden places—the power to protect the Law of his father and his father's father. Saul walked the whole of the way back to his residence with a growing sense of excitement. He would visit the High Priest in the morning at the Temple before the Sanhedrin went to session. He was confident that Caiaphas would grant him the power to finally arrest those who dared to speak of the disgraced Nazarene. As he settled in and prepared to go to sleep in his own soft bed, only one troubling thought found a path to intrude upon his contentment—the look that had come upon Stephen's face just before he died.

The three men crouched behind the crude, square entrance to an underground cistern that held the overflow waters of heavy rains. The tallest of the three, Jacob, peered over the top of the stonework with the focus of a desert hawk circling above an unfortunate mouse. His alert eyes squinted for accuracy under the shade of his bushy black eyebrows. Crouching back down, he spoke quietly to his brother Isaac and his master, "Six have entered, but no one since dusk."

Saul stood upright and shifted a scroll from one hand to the other. "It's time. Alert the others, Isaac."

The balding and square shouldered Isaac scampered away from Saul and Jacob with short, powerful steps that sent the dust of the street flying about his thick ankles. Jacob could see him above those walking in the fading light of the street and watched his brother motion for a small contingent of Temple Police to follow him to a known home. "They are in place," said the sharp eyed Jacob, "it is the third house on the left. It is the home of Nicolas from Antioch, and we should find at least five other followers of the Nazarene in this house."

Saul walked with an arrogant air of authority in the direction of the well built abode. Upon arriving at the entrance, well lit by the light of an oil lantern, he stood back and gave a signal for the police to enter without announcement, and waited for the six worshipers to be thrown at his feet. His right hand held a scroll inscribed with an official decree dictated by the Head Priest, Caiaphas, which gave him the authority to conduct that raid, and all others. This was the fourth home in which they had entered since the previous Sabbath, and the news of havoc he and his men were causing among the community of believers had swept through Jerusalem.

Many of the followers of the Way had fled the capital in fright, but he would eventually hunt them down like a mother searching for lice in the head of a child. There would be no place to hide. No mercy, no rest, until all of Judea and Samaria would be picked clean of these vermin. Only the apostles were safe from the decree he held in his hand, as Caiaphas had instructed him to leave them be, in deference to their extraordinary popularity. "Still," he laughed to himself, "what good are preachers without their congregations? What good are generals without their troops? Once their sheep are scattered, I will go after the shepherds, with the good Caiaphas' permission, and rid our people, once and for all, of this oozing infection."

Saul's amusing reverie was interrupted by the sound of six people, four men and two women, being forcefully dragged through the front door of the home by the police and then pushed down in the dust beneath his rigid stance. Not a single one of the captives spoke, but the air was filled with the shouts and orders of the agitated guards. Saul did not even look down at the accused, but carefully unrolled the scroll to read it aloud. This was the law. "By the order of the High Priest," he spoke out in pitched voice, "you are being arrested for worshiping in the name of Jesus of Nazareth, an outlawed preacher who was executed on orders of the Roman Procurator, Pontius Pilate." He still did not look downward, and instead turned to Jacob to say,

"Take them to the prison."

"Sir, may I speak to you?" said a man on the ground, who tried to rise from his knees to address Saul. A swift boot from a policeman sent him sprawling down upon his chest, but he continued from a prone position, one elbow in the dirt. "I am Nicolas, the owner of this home. I cannot deny that we are followers of the Way, and were worshiping in His name, but I ask you for mercy for the two women here. Please, sir, let them go and we shall take their punishments upon ourselves."

"What foolish courage!" he thought. "How can these scums be so disrespectful to me, an appointed officer of the Sanhedrin? What did the preacher say to them that gives them such misplaced mettle? I should have him beaten at this very spot for his insolence." Saul knelt down so that his face was directly in front of Nicolas' face. The guards stood ready to pounce upon the accused and beat him unmercifully if he so much as even lifted a hand in defense. Saul regarded Nicolas with rapt awareness. Where he expected to see fear in Nicolas's eyes, he saw only the pleading for mercy. Where he expected to see a tremble in his lips, he saw only resoluteness. And where he expected to hear an ever so slight quaking of fear in the voice of the accused, he heard only acceptance, even love. And so it took Saul a moment to gather his wits and give his answer in absolute accordance with the Law. He took a few more moments to search his own thoughts to say what must be said for Nicolas and the other five to hear in certainty. He screamed, "No mercy!" Then Saul turned his back upon the accused who were roughly brought up to their feet and shoved in the direction of the prison. He had no interest in seeing them placed in their fetid cells. He could leave that responsibility to his men, Jacob and Isaac, and the police. His task was clear—to find the others who worshiped in the name of the man whose words threatened the Law and their way of life. He was to find them in the shadows of their hiding places and bring them to justice under the Law.

꧁꧂

aul sat respectfully next to the High Priest. "Thank you, Caiaphas," he said, "we shall leave for Damascus at first light tomorrow."

The High Priest smiled at the intensity of his dedicated appointee. "You will find those papers to be in perfect order. You will have the unquestionable right to search any synagogue in Damascus for those belonging to the Way, and bring them back to Jerusalem for trial. Still, young man, you might want to take a bit more time to gather your provisions for the trip. It takes eight days, at best, to reach Damascus, and one must pack the camels with plenty of water and food."

"With all due respect, my Lord," answered Saul, "I am anxious to begin the journey. My men, Jacob and Isaac, have been gathering our provisions for the trip. We are ready to leave at first light."

"Well, then I tell you to go with God. May the Almighty guide you through the desert on a safe journey," blessed Caiaphas. "Your accomplishments here in the capital have been extraordinary— save the Twelve, and a few protected men of wealth, you have rid this city of the Nazarenes and scattered the rest to other lands."

Saul rose and bowed deeply to the High Priest. He looked about the ornate office and recalled their initial meeting here in that very room, when Caiaphas had pulled him from his studies with Rabbi Gamaliel in the spring of the previous year. From the time of his appointment, he had become a man of great power who commanded respect among his brethren, and sent a dagger of fear to the disciples of the Nazarene. He owed the abundance of his new station to the man to whom he bowed. And now he held close to his breast the papers that would extend his ambition to all of Judea and Samaria. "Your compliments are gracious, but ill founded, my Lord. It was you who recognized the limitations of the positions put forth by your father-in-law, Annas, and the wise Rabban Gamaliel. One cannot allow a snake to slither unchallenged in a home—no, it must be hunted and found so that the head of the serpent can be cut off before it spreads its poison to others. You must take credit for knowing this is so, Caiaphas, and having the courage to lead us to victory."

Eight days later, as the desert sun ascended to its highest spot in the sky during the noon hour, Saul and his two men began to notice the greening of the desert vegetation, a harbinger of the arrival to the city of Damascus. Soon, they would be settled in the city at the home of their friend, Judas, rested and ready to present their papers to the leaders of the city's most prominent synagogues. Saul was confident that he would be received by the leaders as a staunch defender of the Law. Surely, his reputation as a ruthless persecutor of the followers of the Way had already made that journey in the telling mouths of the frightened Nazarenes who had fled to Damascus to escape their inevitable capture in Jerusalem. "And now," he was thinking, "I am chasing them down in Damascus to bring them home in chains. Can you imagine their surprise when I enter into the synagogues and snatch those who dare to speak in the name of the criminal?"

"I am relishing a fine meal, Master, as soon as we put these camels to stable," cried out the portly Isaac, who had slightly thinned his belly by walking in the unrelenting heat. "And I must say, a fine cup of Judas' wine would not be spilled upon his floor!"

Saul laughed at the stocky brother's delicious desires while Jacob just shook his head and continued to take the lead in the journey. For eight days now, the angular head of the older brother had swiveled from side to side searching the rolling dunes for bandits. Another perusal of the vistas was empty of men. They were alone. Soon, they would be in Damascus where Jacob could rest his eyes from the strain of constant attention for their safety. The three of them settled into a feverish silence and urged the camels onward by pulling on their ropes, and with clucks of their tongues to finish off the final leg of the journey.

Then, just as the camels began to perk up by suggestion, a brilliant light, a hundred times brighter than the sun, flashed down upon Saul and his men with a vibrating intensity that knocked them off their feet and sent them sprawling into the hot sands. The light spiraled like a desert windstorm to surround Saul and wrap him like burial cloths, bound within its rays. Saul struggled to rise when a voice pierced him to a dark pool deep in his soul and into apprehension, but he still answered, "Who are you, Lord?" in deference to the overwhelming power of the voice and the light.

"I am Jesus, whom you are persecuting," said the voice.

And then Saul understood. All of the pangs of conscience that had goaded him in his relentless pursuit of the disciples became truth. A great knot was untied by the Lord, in a moment that would have taken him a hundred years to unravel. The look upon Stephen's face as he died; the quiet courage of those he had thrown into prisons; the extraordinary acceptance of the Nazarene's gospel by those who worshiped in His Name; the healing of the lame man at the Beautiful Gate. He understood, at last, that to persecute the believers was to persecute the One who now spoke to him as the Lord of all beings. Trembling and astonished, Saul asked, "Lord, what do You want me to do?"

"Surely," Saul thought, as the sands burned through his exposed skin, "I will perish here for my sins against the Way. I shall die as I have acceded to the deaths of others, without mercy." Then he said, "Strike me dead, Lord, it is my deserved fate!"

Then the Lord said to him, "Arise and go into the city, and you will be told what you must do." And the light dissipated and disappeared back into the sky and all that remained was a deathly silence about the caravan.

Saul struggled mightily to his feet. "Jacob, Isaac, did you hear the voice of the Lord? Did you see Him?" he shrieked to his men. Isaac was too frightened to reply but Jacob answered in time, "We heard a voice, but could not understand the words. A light knocked us off our feet, but we saw no one. Are you all right, Master?"

Saul brought his hands to his eyes to wipe off the sand that covered his face. He ground the palms of his hands in freeing circles into his eyes so that he could clear them of the sharp specks of sand. But, when he opened his eyes to see his men, he saw no one. He was blind. All about him was darkness. A rising fear seized his throat, but his steely resolve held on to force him to accept his circumstance. "I am blind, as blind in sight as I once was to the Spirit," he said to himself. "This is my just punishment; my life had been spared by Jesus, but my eyes have been taken in payment for all that I have done; for all that I failed to see."

"No, Jacob," Saul answered, "I am not; I was blinded by the light. Please, come and help me, and guide me into the city."

So the two men hustled over to aid their master and led him by hand into Damascus. The compliant camels followed the three men in obedience until they arrived at the home of their friend Judas. Isaac went to board the lumbering beasts into the stable while Jacob led Saul, with Judas' assistance, into a room in the coolest part of the home. They placed the exhausted Saul into a bed and lit a candle to illuminate the room.

For three days and three nights, Saul neither ate nor drank as he sat in the cool air without sight. The brothers slept in an adjoining room and checked on their master often while imploring him to eat, or at least take a sip of water. Saul refused all sustenance. He spent the whole of every waking moment trying to assuage his guilt over what he had done as the chief prosecutor of the followers of the Way. Often, he cried out in pain over what he had wrought. There were screams of terror. Even his sleep was tortured as visions and dreams cascaded down upon him in colors too vivid to have ever been seen by his rightful eyes. Nightmares tore at the rigid strands of his self constructed sanity that had so often served him in the past. And so finally, he did what all men do when they are challenged beyond the comfort of food and drink, beyond the soothing nature of their earthly position or calming habits, to a place where all has changed in the wake of one life altering event. The last thing left on the far side of despair. He prayed.

n the modest section of Damascus, where homes were built close enough together to steal each other's light, there lived a man named Ananias, who was of very good reputation and a disciple of Jesus of Nazareth. He was a pious man, respected by all of the Israelites who made Damascus their home. This humble believer had been to the Festival of Weeks in Jerusalem and had witnessed the stirring words of Peter on the day of Pentecost. He had seen the lame man healed and leaping about in joy and praise with his own eyes, and had repented of his sins and immersed himself in a water baptism in the hands of the young disciple, John. On that morning, he was asleep upon his cot in a narrow room with a window that would announce the eastern rising sun. He was a good man, content with his station in life and a devoted follower of Jesus of Nazareth, the Risen Christ. In the early morning, where slowly awakening sleep and dreams swim together like childhood friends, Ananias received a vision from His Lord, who called out to him, "Ananias."

And he said, "Here I am, Lord."

And the Lord said to him, "Arise and go to the street called Straight, and inquire at the house of Judas for one called Saul of Tarsus, for behold, he is praying. And in a vision, he has seen a man named Ananias coming in and putting his hands on him, so that he might receive his sight."

A bolt of fear shot through Ananias, but he was committed, heart and soul, to his Lord. So he answered, "Lord, I have heard from many about this man, how much harm he has done to Your saints in Jerusalem. And hear that he has the authority, from the chief priests, to bind all who call on Your name."

But the Lord said to him, "Go, for he is a chosen vessel of Mine to bear My name before Gentiles, kings, and the children of Israel. For I will show him how many things he must suffer for My name's sake."

So Ananias shook the sleep from his awakening eyes and stood up from his slender cot to dress in his robe and sandals. He knew the street well, for it ran the length of the city from one end to the other. He would allow the Lord to guide him to someone on Straight Street who might know of the house of Judas where the prosecutor from Jerusalem rested in darkness. He moved quickly through the uneven and winding, cramped passages of the city of Damascus before speaking with a shopkeeper opening his place of business on the appointed street. The shopkeeper knew of Judas and where he lived. A few moments later, Ananias stood outside the wooden door, offered one final prayer to the Lord, and knocked in the confidence of his assignment. He knocked in full faith, but not without a fear of the one he was coming to visit.

A tall, serious man with a long, thin beard opened the door to Ananias. "May I help you," said Jacob, answering for Judas who had left at first light.

"I am here to see Saul of Tarsus. Please take me to him, sir," said the disciple with such assuredness that Jacob merely opened the door to allow an unimpeded entrance, and turned to show the way without even inquiring as to why Ananias was here to see his master. Jacob led Ananias down a long corridor to a private room at the far end where a candle twinkled a sliver above its own pool of wax. Ananias entered the room and saw the notorious

Saul, now as quiet as a Sabbath meal, sitting on the edge of the bed with his head held high above a straight back. Saul did not speak. He waited graciously. So Ananias crossed the room to where the red headed man sat in silence and, laying his hands upon his eyes, said, "Brother Saul, the Lord Jesus, who appeared to you on the road as you came, has sent me, so that you may receive your sight and be filled with the Holy Spirit." First, tears fell from Saul's open, but blinded, eyes and then something like scales trickled down upon his lap, and immediately his sight was restored.

Saul blinked the new light into his restored eyes, which searched for Ananias' face. Gently, lovingly, Ananias lifted Saul to his feet and held him by the arm, and they walked slowly toward a table where a bowl of soft dates stood next to some bread and water. Saul took a tiny piece of the bread and dipped it into the water before bringing it to his mouth. It was his first food and drink in three days, and one bite brought him a measure of strength. The second brought a touch more. When he had consumed a few more, and tore at the skin of a soft date to suck out some of the rich juice, he spoke to Ananias for the first time, in gratefulness. "Thank you, my brother, and praise be to the Lord Jesus, who has restored my sight and strength."

"Now, come with me to be baptized, calling on His name," said Ananias. And together they walked to the edge of the city to a pool of brimming water that stood at the highest entrance of the city. Saul took off his sandals and stepped into the cooling waters. Ananias followed and walked the fierce persecutor slowly to the deeper center. He took Saul by his shoulders and shouted out for all to hear in the heavens, "I baptize you in the name of the Lord Jesus Christ, buried in the likeness of His death, raised in the likeness of His resurrection." As Saul was thrust down into the healing waters, a thousand images flooded through his vision; a kiss from his father leaving him in Jerusalem to learn at the feet of Rabbi Gamaliel; the Latin inscription upon the seal that closed the tomb of the crucified Nazarene; the blood that trickled down Annas' thumb when he pricked it upon a thorn in his garden so many days previous; the sharp stitched line of a luxurious chair where the dark wood met the silken fabric in the home of Joseph of Arimathea; the beautiful face of Stephen when he first heard him speak on the steps of the synagogue; Peter and John and the lame man leaping about with the same joy that he felt now, immersed in that cleansing water. No hatred. No zealotry. No hint of superiority. Peace. Only a single image burned into his soul in the middle of that light of a hundred suns, in the middle of that voice calling out to him in the desert—Jesus, the Messiah; The Christ. He had seen the Lord. And then Saul was yanked back above the surface with water flying off the tips of his red curls. The rigidity of his former ways floated away in the swirling waters, but his relentless passion remained beating in his heart. Not for a set of rules to govern all aspect of one's life, but to a way of living in the forgiveness of one's sins. Love in true kindness without envy; patience in tribulation. Rejoicing in hope. Being steadfast in prayer. Seeking not the revenge that is the Lord's. Loving your neighbor as yourself. Putting on Christ as his armor and a light for others to see that love never fails. Never. It endures all things. He prayed, "Yes, I feel the passion to take this unearned gift, this incredible grace, to the four corners of the earth. I now give my life, the force that roars inside of me, my zealous nature, my knowledge, and all of my being to you Lord. I am free. Converted. Released. I am free to take of the bread of life, saved by Your blood. Everyone will hear of You in whatever language they speak, and I shall call out Your name, wherever I go, until my death. This I promise You in this wetness, my immersion. Thank you, my Lord."

Ananias held the trembling Saul in his arms. He pushed him away at arm's length to see the Holy Spirit as He filled him. At once, Ananias knew that the assignment given to him by the Lord had been completed. His work was over. For in his arms was the most ruthless, vicious persecutor of Jesus and His disciples, but who would now accept His divine commission to spread the Gospel of the Lord Jesus to all of the Gentiles, the kings and rulers, and to all the children of Israel. He would bring the good news to the world. The great persecutor would now become the great proclaimer of the gospel of Jesus Christ. Yes, the man that stood dripping in his arms would not be denied. He had been converted, whirled about to preach the message of Christ. In the morning, Ananias would send the word back to the Twelve in Jerusalem about what had happened on the road to Damascus to the man most feared by those who follow the Way.

"Ananias, thank you," said a serene Saul, "I am a changed man. God has given me a new mission in life. I am now one with the Lord Jesus Christ."

"Then go, my son," replied Ananias, before kissing Saul in peace upon the cheek, "Go with the peace of the Lord." But Saul did not hear that blessing. His eyes were looking beyond Ananias to the lands that lay to the east, Parthia and India, and then to the west, to Rome and Gaul and Hispania. He looked across the scorching desert in one direction, and the frolicking sea in the other; to faraway lands and kings and emperors and to the people who did not know of the One born in Galilee; to serving his Lord and Savior and bringing the story of hope, and the good news of salvation, to a hungry world ready to accept The Gift. The Grace. The Peace. Forevermore.

Epilogue

AD 95, Patmos

A personal letter from the Apostle John; written by candlelight from his cave while in exile in Patmos, to his friend Ignatius, a leader in the Church in Ephesus.

My beloved Ignatius,

To you, my brave child, I write from a darkened cave in Patmos, where the Lord has sent me for my final days. Perhaps you will read this letter after I have left you, but do not grieve for me. For I greet you today with the contentment of living in the peace, grace and mercy of the Lord Jesus Christ, a love that warms me even in this bitter chill. I long to join Him in Heaven, my Light and Savior; to be next to Him again in all of His glory and to lay my head upon His rightful breast. And yet, my time to die has not arrived for He speaks to me in nightly dreams and revelations whenever I close my eyes to rest.

I am the last of the Twelve who lives. Each of the others have died at the hands of our persecutors and enemies, proclaiming their faith with great courage to the very moment of their deaths. Peter, our rock, crucified by Nero with his head pointing downward to the ground, for he did not feel worthy to die in the same manner as our Lord. His brother Andrew, crucified on an X shaped cross in Patras, with the name of Jesus proclaimed from his lips for the whole of the day of his death. James, my own brother, and the first to be martyred among us, losing his head to King Herod Agrippa in the forty-fourth year after the birth of the Lord. Thomas, attacked and killed by a group of sages on a hill in Chennai in India. The guileless one, Bartholomew, skinned alive for refusing to worship the pagan gods of Armenia. Matthew, his body speared to death as his blood spilled upon Persian soil. Phillip, crucified in Hierapolis alongside his sister Mariamne, preaching fervently from the cross unto his last breath. James the Lesser, crucified in lower Egypt before they sawed his body into pieces and fed them to wild dogs. Simon the Zealot, sawn in two alive, from head to toe and killed alongside a beaten Thaddeus in Suanir. The last disciple, Matthias, brought among us by the revelation of a thrown lot, murdered by lance and ax in Colchis. And please let us not forget Paul, the Apostle to the Gentiles, who survived so many plots to murder him, only to be finally beheaded in Rome by Nero's men, the execution of choice for Roman citizens. All of them—tortured and killed for their ceaseless faith in our Lord Jesus Christ.

And yet, my precious child, the Church grows in strength and numbers. I am confident that you are a living example of our Lord in our community of Ephesus. It brings me joy in this darkness to think of your walk with our Lord and your influence among those who have just begun to experience the gift that He gave to us with His sacrifice. Just as the apostles died while preaching the gospel to others, so shall you proclaim your devoted faith to those who yearn to be free of the clutches of everlasting sin. Stand tall, my son, and speak clearly for we were commissioned to take the good news to the four corners of the Earth. The commission extends to you! Be not afraid to speak in His name, for what is this life but a flash of lightning against the one we will spend in eternity with Him. Speak and be vulnerable for it is at the moment of full vulnerability that one finds the greatest of all strengths. Never forget the strength of our Lord who prayed for His tormentor's forgiveness even as they hammered his arms outstretched onto a wooden cross. If you love in His example in the face of hatred, then you will have touched the Kingdom of Heaven and a place shall be prepared for you. No evil, no devious scheme to destroy and murder, no king nor power in all of the lands, can touch the everlasting love of the Risen Christ.

My time is drawing near, my child. Heed my words, Ignatius, and proclaim the truth of the gospel. You must carry on our work. If I do not lay my eyes upon your beautiful face again, know that I left this world in full surrender to my Lord and Master, Jesus Christ. And know that I left with a smile upon my wrinkled face. Tell my little children to love the Lord Almighty and one another. It is our Lord's most precious request of us and if this is done, it is enough. Live, my son, and love, for it has been revealed to me in the middle of these long, cold nights. I have seen it.

He lives, and He will come again.

Your faithful servant, John.

Thirty Three, The Story of Hope

Major Character Glossary

Joseph of Arimathea—A well respected merchant of some wealth who was a member of the ruling Sanhedrin. Joseph was the owner of the tomb near Golgotha into which he placed the body of Jesus of Nazareth before the onset of dusk on the day of His crucifixion.

Nicodemus—A Pharisee and a member of the Sanhedrin who assisted Joseph of Arimathea in the preparation of Jesus' body for proper burial in a accordance with Jewish Law.

John (The Young Disciple)—A fisherman who left his vocation to become a disciple of John the Baptist. He and his brother, James, became the first two disciples of the Rabbi Jesus after His baptism by John the Baptist. He became an apostle and is credited with the writing of the Book of Revelation.

James the Disciple—The older brother of John.

Thomas the Disciple—A dour but deeply committed disciple/apostle of Jesus of Nazareth. He is often referred to as Doubting Thomas.

Mother Mary—The Virgin Mother of Jesus of Nazareth.

Aunt Mary—The sister of Mother Mary and the wife of Cleopas.

Mary Magdalene (The Magdalene, Miriam)—A devoted follower of Jesus who accompanied Him and the Twelve disciples in the year before His crucifixion. She is often referred to as the "Apostle to the Apostles."

Saul (Paul)—A formally educated Pharisee from Tarsus. His primary teacher was the revered Rabbi Gamaliel who instructed the young student on the history of the twelve tribes of Israel and the Torah. Paul (Greek name) enjoyed the rights and privileges of Roman citizenship.

Pontius Pilate—The Prefect for the Roman territory of Judea in the years AD 26 to AD 33.

Caiaphas—The High Priest of the Sanhedrin originally appointed by the Roman Prefect, Valerius Gratus, in the year AD 18. A Sadduccee, he served as the High Priest and chairman of the Sanhedrin until the year AD 37.

Annas—The previous High Priest before Caiaphas who was his son-in-law. A powerful and influential figure in Jerusalem with close relationships with the ruling Romans.

Rabbi Gamaliel—a tremendously respected teacher of the Jewish Law and the primary teacher for Saul of Tarsus. His scholarship and intellectual prowess earned him the honored title of Rabban. Known as one of the greatest teachers of the Hillel School in the annals of Judiasm.

Stephen—A Hellenist and devotee of Jesus of Nazareth. He was known as a man of great beauty and charisma who exhibited the ability to effect signs and wonders.

Acknowledgements

In Gratitude

First and foremost, I extend my deepest gratitude to our Managing Partner at 33 Hope, Kirk Berendes, who came to see me in October of 2008 to recount a family story. He had taken two of his young sons to see Mel Gibson's "The Passion of the Christ", the vivid, cinematic portrayal of the last twelve hours of Jesus of Nazareth's life before His death by crucifixion. Both of the children had been enthralled by the movie and one of them, Christian, had turned to Kirk and asked, "But, daddy, what happened next?" It was that simple question posed by a child that became the core basis for this book and the inspiration for our entire 33 Hope Project which can be reviewed at: www.33Hope.com.

To our brilliant, entertainment attorney and treasured 33 Hope Partner, William Whitacre. There would be little hope for 33 Hope without you. Thank you for your precise ability to structure our partnerships and key affiliations in cooperative rhythm with our mutual goals. Thank you for showing us a path to the summit. But most of all, Bill, thank you for your sparkling personality and for never forgetting the fundamental inspiration behind our negotiations.

To our creative partner at 33 Hope, Richard Hayes, and his amazing team at DigitalLightBridge led by Chris Whitten and Paul Tejera. Thank you for nailing our graphics on our first day together. Rich, we remain in constant need of your spiritual maturity—you are a man who has dedicated his life to the Lord

188

Jesus Christ and we appreciate that your eyes never waver from that truth. You inspire us that all things are possible with Jesus Christ, by the way in which you live and work.

To our National Brand Consultant and Publishing Partners, the masterful team of Sound Enterprises, Inc. To their CEO, Brad Damon and his partner, Jim Caviezel, the actor who has lain down his substantial power and influence at the foot of the Cross. And especially to their seasoned marketing pro, Rodney Hatfield, for your experience and your invaluable friendship. You were smart enough to guide us gently forward, step by step, and wise enough to make it seem as if each step was our own idea. And thank you, my dear friend, for asking the original question on that sofa so many months ago, that helped us to discern our evangelical soul.

To the maestro, Dale Oliver of OTM Production, the composer of our 33 Hope Anthem—"He's Alive." Thank you for placing our song in the voices of Jupiter Wind. We will do so much together in the future, my friend, as we love the music that flows from your patient and peaceful heart.

To Raul Fonseca, my Biblical mentor and a scriptural expert on the life and words of Jesus Christ. You taught me to read the threads in the Bible as they weave their way from Genesis to Revelation. Thank you for learning Greek and Hebrew and diligently working with me to seek exactly what Jesus said in context to the original languages and cultural mores in the year AD 33. You have a very special gift, my friend, bestowed upon you in Spirit by the Lord. Thank you for unwrapping it so patiently with me.

To my editor, Lee Fredrickson of 21st Century Press, for your exacting nature and patience. Thank you for speaking the King's English with such precision and in full spirit. You are a true pro and I extend my full appreciation to you for having mastered your craft and for smoothing the rough edges of this manuscript into a cohesive flow.

To Scott Matirne, the Voice of 33 Hope. Thank you for your Louisiana passion and for getting up every day to pray for us in the early dawn. Be careful what you pray for, though—God may grant your entreaty in totality!

To Phil Gilliam for your vision and truly evangelical heart. Friend, we shall look to "cloud" this world together in His name. Thank you for instructing us on the unlimited potential to communicate and build community in the New World.

To the Swedish Saxophonist, Johan Stengard, for the gift of your lyrical music to 33 Hope. We are excited to work with you in collaboration to sing to God.

And to Lori, Zachary, Christian, Tyler and Jill Berendes, Jean Berendes, Ed and Beverly Flom, Janette Anderson, Tony and Julie Pizzo, Mark and Melissa Flom, Jeannette King Flom, David and Lauren Hicks, Gay Whitacre, Lisa Hayes, Beth Hirsch, Barbara Matirne, Michael and Buck Berendes, Lou Lamphier, Stuart Navarro, Robert Sanford, George Cline, Mike and Mary Beth Finster, Cristobal Krusen and Doug Maddox, Father Tom Spillett, Father Tom Madden, Rob and Tom Faw, Bert and Lorraine Kaplan, Robert Gross, the Harrington family, Brian McNulty, Brian Weiler, Tim Barber, Paul Akre, Doug King, John and Melissa Twomey, Jim Burt, Robert Thomas, Bob Collins, Anne Quinlan, Sandy Holcomb-Wahl, Teresa Bain Ferrell, Larry Smith, Mary Dorris, Tom Pugh, Terry Mulvey, Drew Orye, Will Wiard, and the entire gang at the 2009 Clearwater Beach Summer Project (Campus Crusade for Christ). Each of you know our gratitude.

And lastly, in memoriam to Kirk's father, Floyd Berendes, who passed away during the writing of this book. Your servant's heart and enthusiastic personality lives on in every initiative that we undertake. Please watch out for us and work with God to clear the path upon which we hope to tread.

Thirty Three was never our project or my book. Since our inception, we have been divinely guided by God in each ordered step. He brought to us likehearted, talented individuals at the precise time in which we needed them to complete each step and continues to do so as we move forward with our bold initiatives. It has been our humble honor to stay in assignment to His will. And so, most of all, we thank Him for each illumination and for the precious Gift of His son, Jesus, the Risen Christ!